Aug 17

THE MINOR OUTSIDER

TED MCDERMOTT

AN IMPRINT OF PUSHKIN PRESS

ONE
an imprint of Pushkin Press
71–75 Shelton Street,
London WC2H 9JQ

Copyright © Ted McDermott, 2016

First published by ONE in 2016

1 3 5 7 9 8 6 4 2

ISBN 978 0992918 27 9

Text designed and typeset by Tetragon, London
Printed and bound by CPI Group (UK) Ltd, Croydon, CRO 4YY

www.pushkinpress.com/one

For Shawn

On a sunny summer weekday afternoon, Ed rode his bike to a head shop called Piece of Mind and bought a one-hitter that looked like a realistic sculpture of a cigarette. Ed was twenty-eight years old and single. He was thin and just over six feet tall. He had dark hair cut short and he wore round wire-rim glasses, cut-off khaki shorts, and a long-sleeved collared shirt. Ed was enrolled in a graduate creative writing program, which meant he taught one section of composition a semester and took workshops and other easy classes, but now he was five weeks into a four-month summer vacation and he had nothing he had to do. He'd been rolling joints for himself, but he thought he'd be able to moderate better how much he smoked if he had a small bowl. He'd never bought a bowl. Never in the seventeen years since he'd started smoking weed, as a sixth grader. Now he had one. Now what?

Ed biked through the quaint downtown and across the bridge that spanned the river that ran through the little city, which occupied a valley surrounded by rolling green mountains. Starker, darker mountains existed in every distance. From here, on his bike, on the bridge, he could see at once so many places he'd never been, would never go. He could see snow on a peak that was thirty miles away, a lone pine tree tiny on a ridge without a trail, what might or might not be a tent set up above a black scree.

This was in Missoula, Montana, a town as orderly and idyllic as the landscape a model train loops through, a town of some 60,000 people, a town eight hours from the nearest major city, Seattle. Together, these qualities—Missoula's self-containment, its smallness, its isolation, its layered and intangible landscape—shrunk his range of concern and facilitated an ease he'd never felt elsewhere. Still, he was suspicious of it, this ease: life, for him, was a commodity, and he was frugal.

After the bridge, Ed took a gravel path that ran along the river's bank. He stopped when he came to a little trail that led through some tangled brush, to a sandy beach where he liked to swim when the river was lower. Now, though, the river was still raging from winter, from the snowpack that was still melting down from the mountains. It was June.

He took the trail toward the water, laid his bike down on the sand, sat on a log, and looked back to check that he was hidden from view. He was—but on the other side of the river, at the top of the high and steep bank, there was a Taco John's franchise. The back of a Taco John's franchise. There was a blue dumpster and a rusted a/c unit and some half-hearted small-town graffiti sprayed on the cinder-block side of the building and there was a drive-thru window and he wondered if the employees could see him through it. Maybe. Maybe not. Either way, they'd be too far away to matter, so he packed the fake cigarette and got high. But not too high. Just high enough to make everything a little less like it was.

Ed looked at the river. It traveled as fast as it could but it went nowhere. *I'm like that*, he thought. Then he

thought, *I'm high*. Then he got up, got on his bike, continued
down the path, and crossed the river again, this time via
a pedestrian bridge, and rode through a hotel parking lot
and waited at a stoplight and rode under an interstate that
sounded like the river, except amplified. Ed turned off the
busy road as soon as he could, into a dirt alley. He passed
backyards. He passed garages and grass and a trampoline
and a wooden boat overturned on a pair of sawhorses. He
came out onto a street, turned again, and went as far as he
could—a few blocks—to where the pavement dead-ended
at a trailhead, where a sign provided information about
invasive weeds.

Ed locked his bike to a young tree and started walking.
The trail led to a giant "L" made of poured concrete and set
on the side of one of the green mountains that defined the
valley. This mountain was Mount Jumbo. The next mountain
over, Mount Sentinel, had an "M" the same size. "M" stood for
the name of the town or for the name of the state university
in the town or for both, depending who you asked. But the
"L" stood for a local high school called Loyola Sacred Heart,
whose mascot was the Breakers, which pleased him, made
him proud that the people here—a group that for the past
year had included him—were so casually clever.

The mountain was relatively small, but the hike was still
hard. The ground was green grass and loose rock and dry
dirt, and every step he took made a little mess of the earth. It
took a while but he got there and sat down exhausted on the
white-painted concrete, beside a plaque that commemorated
a student named John Tyler Howard who'd died a few years
before, at the age, he calculated from the birth and death
dates, of fifteen. No cause was recorded.

Ed looked out at the mountains that made the valley that held the town. He saw the little Division I-AA (or whatever it was called now) football stadium and the crummy dorm that was Missoula's tallest building and the interstate that would take you all the way to the ocean, if you wanted to leave, and the river that would take you there, too. In theory, at least. Surely something would stop you before you got very far. And Ed saw someone coming up the path. Two people. He saw them come closer and he saw, when they were close, that they were female and that he knew one of them, that she was a twenty-four-year-old nonfiction writer in the program whose name was Melanie and who, according to his friend Dave who'd had a workshop with her, exclusively wrote personal essays about how her mother was an unsuccessful folk singer who drove her daughters all over the country in a conversion van, playing gigs that barely paid. He didn't recognize the other girl, but as Ed watched them approach, he saw she was blond and that she wore a light-blue tank top and short jean shorts and that she was thin and that she lagged behind Melanie a little.

He said hey to them when they were close and they looked up at him, out of breath.

Melanie gave him a little wave and said, "Oh, hey," and stopped before him with her hands on her hips. She was wholesome, plain. The kind of girl who's so sincere and has such a bad sense of humor that they're difficult to talk to, like an aunt.

"How's it going?" Melanie said.

"Good. It's good. Nice day, huh?"

Then the other girl arrived and looked at him and breathed heavily, with an eager and shy smile that seemed to mean she was relieved to have arrived, and Ed saw she was disarmingly lovely. He wanted badly to be disarmed.

"This is Taylor," Melanie said. "She's a first year."

By this, Melanie meant that Taylor would be starting their same graduate writing program in the fall. Their program was like a high school where angst had been replaced with irony.

Taylor's skin was pale and her cheeks were flushed pink and her hair was long and blond and curled with a curling iron, he could tell, and her eyes were green and bright and the only way he'd be able to think of her later would be as a series of adjectives—girlish, pretty, radiant—but right now he was nervous and couldn't think anything.

Ed introduced himself, put out his hand. Taylor shook it. Her hand was warm, and Ed felt shy, holding it. He let go and asked her where she was from.

"California."

"Yeah? Where?"

"Oh, Southern California. The Mojave Desert. Kinda between LA and Vegas."

"Is Death Valley in the Mojave Desert?"

"I think so," Taylor said. "Pretty far north of where I'm from though."

"I had a step-grandmother who was a fire lookout out there." Ed hoped this would make him seem interesting and a maybe a shade blue collar, which is to say authentic, which of course he wasn't, even though it was true, this fact about his step-grandmother, Joan. "But what would even burn in a desert?"

Melanie laughed a little, in an attempt at agreement, but Taylor looked at him mystified, like she wasn't sure what he meant, what the joke was supposed to be, and she didn't answer. Ed tried to convey with his expression that he didn't know either, but he doubted this came across. He felt embarrassed, dumb. The three of them made bland introductory conversation for a little longer, and then Melanie said they should get going.

"Maybe we'll see you later," Melanie said.

"Maybe."

Ed watched them walk back down the mountain. Before following them, he had to wait until they were way ahead, since it would be awkward to catch up and run into them again, so he lay back on the "L," felt the sun and felt a shock of pain shoot through his arm, into his hand, where it echoed within the elements of his anatomy. His bones, his muscles, his nerves, and his blood. Or felt like it did. It was a common feeling, this shock. It happened every night when Ed lay in bed—except when he was drunk—and at other times, too, seemingly at random. It—the shock—originated in the golf-ball sized tumor that had been growing on the inside of his bicep for nearly three years. The tumor sent pain into him but he pretended it wasn't there, inside him, harming him.

The tumor was like the millions of children starving in Africa: too alarming to think about. It wasn't like that: he could go to a doctor tomorrow and do something about it. But he didn't. He lay on that letter, on that mountain, and he thought about Taylor, about how beautiful she was and about what she might be like and about how it might be to touch her and about how she might respond and about how she might become his and about how that would be, how perfect it would be, how jealous everyone would be, how proud he would be, and meanwhile cancer spread through his body. Or so he believed.

2

E d had first noticed the tumor while living in Normal, Illinois, and working in marketing for a prestigious small press that published experimental literature in translation. The press's offices were in a windowless warehouse surrounded by a chair factory, a trailer park, a cornfield, and an interstate. His job was to garner attention for the obscure and dense books they published and to convince bookstores to buy them. The authors were from places like Romania and South Korea, and their books were difficult to read and almost impossible to sell.

Ed worked at one of those glowing-blue iMacs from the late '90s. It had a round mouse. He shared an office with a man who used hair gel to conceal his bald spot. The press's director was maniacal and paranoid. The director didn't even allow his employees a lunch break, much less a vacation or health insurance. Ed could've quit at any time but, like all of his coworkers, he'd been convinced that the press's mission of making commercially unviable books available was noble and necessitated sacrifice, so he remained.

The job was miserable but the town was worse. In fact, there were two towns, Bloomington and Normal, which were connected and separate, like an amoeba midway through meiosis. Most locals called the combination "Blormal" but he preferred "Normington," as he believed it better captured the particular form of bland despair inherent to the place. The town was all dirty grocery stores and faltering strip malls and brand new subdivisions spilling out into the surrounding fields of ten-foot-tall corn. The town's primary employer was a major insurance company, and there was something actuarial about the local population. People there were guided by a cruel kind of caution. Nothing ever happened and everyone conspired to keep it that way.

He'd moved to Normington because everyone else he knew from college was moving to Brooklyn or Portland or going on tour with their band, and Ed wanted to do something different, something interesting. It turned out, though, that he spent most of his time working in marketing, getting drunk, getting high, and pining for his college girlfriend, who was the only person he'd ever slept with and who'd left him for a guy she met in one of her scientific illustration classes. After enough pining, Ed convinced himself he still loved her and sent her embarrassingly "poetic" emails that he imagined might win her back. They didn't and he started sleeping with a girl who had patches of blond facial hair on her cheeks and her chin. Her facial hair wasn't immediately obvious but it was the only thing you could see when you saw her, once you saw it. She was thin, though, and she liked to be choked and otherwise fucked roughly and he was angry about his ex-girlfriend's rejection, so he slept with her but rarely hung out with her otherwise. She was a nurse who owned her own home. She worked in the ER. Her name was Rachel.

It was one morning at Rachel's house, while showering before he went to work, that Ed first noticed the tumor. He was soaping up his arm and he felt something hard between the muscles of his bicep. He looked but saw nothing. He pressed his thumb against his skin, in search of it. When he found it, a shock of pain shot down his arm and into his hand, where it swelled and spread until it reached his skin. Then the pain reverberated within his skin. Or that's how it felt. It didn't hurt, exactly, but it was unpleasant.

Ed finished showering, put on the same clothes he'd worn the day before, resolved to ignore the bump until it was gone, left the steamy bathroom, and drove to work. Rachel was already at the hospital, saving someone's life or something, and Ed sat at his iMac in the windowless warehouse, sending emails to lit bloggers about some forthcoming Czech novel the press was reprinting. It was one of those times when you realize how differently we all experience the world and you feel alone.

He spent the next few years like that, though without Rachel: going on with his life and pretending that he'd discovered nothing, even as the tumor grew and sent shocks of pain down his arm with increasing frequency. Eventually, Ed moved to Chicago, where he lived in a studio apartment, dated a plain and cautious girl who was a few years older than him, and worked as the only staff writer at a disreputable regional boating magazine. He made a living writing articles about boat design and boat models and boat manufacturers and boating accessories, but Ed had only been on a boat once, while in high school, on a pontoon, on a huge manmade lake outside of the South Carolina city where he grew up. He also wrote features about places he'd never been, places where Great Lakes boaters might like to go: Ashtabula, Ohio; Quebec City, Quebec; Manitowoc, Wisconsin.

He was good at telling convincing lies. So, in his free time, he wrote a few grotesque and maudlin short stories about retarded children. Ed's sister was retarded, and her life made good material, unlike his, so he used it, used her. With the stories, he applied to a few graduate creative writing programs and only got into one. The one in Missoula.

3

E d lived with a twenty-three-year-old Ohioan who wrote religious poetry and who was also enrolled in the graduate creative writing program. They shared a little house with low ceilings and lots of wood paneling, linoleum, and carpet the color of curdled cream. Ed believed the house was technically a shotgun shack, but he felt that using this term would imply that he was poor and he wasn't poor, even if he didn't make much money, so he just called it a house.

Not only was he not poor, Ed had $82,000. He told no one about this money and barely even admitted he had it to himself: privilege is humiliating because it precludes suffering, which is ennobling. Almost all of the money was invested in stocks, and it was held in an account that he could view online. At least twice a day he logged onto the investment firm's website and checked whether he'd gained or lost since the last time he looked. Yesterday he had $81,982 and last week he had $84,215. It was a number, though, so it was abstract, even when it appeared to be precise.

Before the current recession started, he'd had about a third as much money. His grandmother had left it to him when she died. His grandmother was a Polish Jew who'd fled Hitler and gone to New York, where she married a Russian Jew who owned a linoleum store. Soon after the market crashed in

2008, Ed had bought stock in a computer company with his grandmother's money. When the market bounced back, his shares tripled in price and he profited greatly. The money ensured that he couldn't be poor, unless he indulged extravagantly, which he would never do. Though he did occasionally loan himself a few hundred dollars, when his checking account was especially low, he always paid it back.

Like the other privileged people he knew, Ed was afraid to take his advantage. He didn't want to appear comfortable and therefore aloof from the hard realities of being alive, even though of course he was and even though he did nothing to change that fact. Instead, he elaborated hardship whenever he could. To do otherwise, Ed believed, would be bad for his writing. And writing was a way of imbuing his life with purpose, direction. Writing gave him an aim that was both specific enough to be pursued and so vague that it could never be achieved and, thus, would keep him continually moving forward, toward something: to be a writer. And this sense of progress allowed him to forget where he was actually moving: toward nothing, toward death.

Ed's room was in the back of the house, and all of the room's walls and even, weirdly, its ceiling were painted the same sea-foam green. The room had one big window that looked out on the backyard and the garage and a dirt alley. The only other window was small and near the painted ceiling. It was like a porthole, except rectangular, and it gave the room the tucked away feeling of a berth on a boat. Instead of a dresser, he had a stack of plastic bins his mom had bought for him at Target ten years ago, when he was eighteen and about to live in a dorm room with a kid named Johannes, though he went by Joh, pronounced "Joe." The drawers of the plastic bins were clear, so he could see his clothes folded and stacked inside like the organs of a complicated animal.

When he was home, Ed spent most of his time in his room because his roommate spent most of his time sitting on a futon in the living room, smoking a glass bowl and watching the same scratched *Seinfeld* DVDs over and over and reading Wittgenstein and working on a long prose poem about King Herod, all of which bothered Ed. Ed thought of his roommate as a precocious and entitled child, much as his actual younger brother had actually been when they were kids.

So Ed stayed in his room, smoked his one hitter, and masturbated in the middle of the afternoon as quietly as he could to his idea of how his ideal girl would behave in bed. Obediently. Innocently. Then he read a Belgian novel about the mundane complexity of the modern world. Then he drove to Wendy's. When he was on his way home, eating fries out of the paper bag, his sister called.

"What's up Ellie Bird?"

"Hey," she said. "How's your car doing?"

"It's doing good."

This was how all of their phone conversations started, verbatim. His sister, Ellie, had an IQ of sixty-five. Ellie was three years older than him. She had a boyfriend named Roger who worked in the produce department of a Piggly Wiggly in the South Carolina town where they grew up and where she still lived. The Piggly Wiggly on Devine Street. Ellie lived with their parents and worked in an industrial laundry. She stacked baby blankets that came from various area hospitals. That was her job. She did it for eight hours a day, had done it five days a week for thirteen years. It was something a nun would do. It was a life of penance, but for

her there was no purpose, nothing to repent. At birth she'd
been burdened and now she suffered senselessly, endlessly.
No one knew what had caused her deficiency, but their mother
blamed herself. Specifically, she blamed Ellie's condition on a
urinary tract infection she'd had when she conceived. Based
on no evidence, other than the coincidence of her infection
and her daughter's retardation, their mother believed this
infection caused the defect that caused her daughter to
suffer. To substantiate her belief, she sought the appropriate
evidence. At age thirty-eight, she returned to school to get
her master's degree in epidemiology and study the causes
of mental retardation.

Their mother spent six years seeking a connection. She
got numerous grants and even a non-tenure track position
at the local state university to facilitate her research. She
worked long hours and conducted increasingly outlandish
experiments in search of an answer, but her results were
finally inconclusive and funding eventually stopped coming
through and her position was finally discontinued. Now she
no longer worked, but she said she'd learned something from
her failure: all you can do for the helpless is help them. So
she took care of her daughter.

She drove Ellie to work at 6:40 a.m. and picked her up at
3:20 p.m. She drove Ellie to Special Olympics basketball and
Special Olympics swimming and Aktion Club meetings and
friends' houses and doctor's appointments and grocery stores.
She cooked for her daughter and cleaned up after her and did
her laundry. She held her down on the couch and flossed her
teeth. She checked in on Ellie before she finished showering,
to ensure her hair wasn't still soapy, but it always was, so she
told Ellie to rinse it better. Sometimes, Ellie obeyed.

Ed talked to Ellie as he drove and ate fries. She asked him the same questions she always asked him—What did you do last night? When are you coming home to visit? What did you have for dinner?—and she didn't respond to his answers. She never did. She'd memorized all the empty pleasantries of conversation but she didn't know how to assemble them, what to make of them. She was laconic and distracted. During their conversation, no information was exchanged. He pulled up in front of his house and said, "I'm gonna let you go."

She kept talking and he kept trying to tell her he had to hang up, but she wouldn't take the cue, so he ended the call before she could say goodbye. He loved her automatically, effortlessly, the way you would your child. She was a kind of child.

When Ed went inside, his roommate was sitting at the kitchen table, beneath a cheap chandelier. Only two bulbs weren't burned out.

"What's up?"

His roommate was eating a frozen pizza off the cardboard it came on. "Not much." Only one piece was left. They talked about what they might do later, what they'd been doing earlier, and his roommate said, "I saw that new girl. The cute one. Taylor."

"The blond one?"

"Yeah," his roommate said. "I guess she's super Christian."

"How do you know?"

"She was going to church."

Ed laughed.

"She was all dressed up, in like a conservative dress, but she was still hot. But her boyfriend, he seems like kind of like a dork," his roommate said. "It's weird, but I guess that's how Christians are."

"So does the boyfriend live here?"

"I guess."

Ed went in his room, sat on the bed, and ate, disappointed. He felt rejected, even though he'd made no advance. This, he thought, was indicative of how much he desired her, despite how little he knew about her, despite the fact that all he did know of her—her evangelical, he imagined, devotion to Christ—seemed dumb. In search of an explanation, he tried to align his impressions of Taylor with his impression of Christians in general. He was able to, easily. She'd seemed wholesome and hopeful. Naïve. Wrong somehow about how the world saw her. Too demure for how striking she was. But all of that only made him desire her more deeply, he realized, because his attraction was rooted in his perception of her innocence, which he wanted to exploit. Wanted to but wouldn't, since she had a boyfriend. He tried to think of someone else he might desire but only came up with a certain bartender who treated him like a burden.

When Ed was done eating, he smoked his one hitter and he had this memory, which he remembered often: his sister was in high school and she was as frustrated and pent-up and confused as any teenager but she lacked the government of intellect, so she couldn't console herself, so she would scream and cry in tantrums that could go on for an hour or more and one time she was being unreasonable and weeping at the top of the stairs and their dad, who worked as an economist for the South Carolina Department of Revenue, was trying to calm her but he couldn't and then he reached back and slapped her and you could hear the smack and of course this only made everything worse. His dad must've felt a version of disappointment then that Ed would never understand.

Ed's father was the kindest man he knew, but Ed was suspicious of this kindness, suspected that his father was disguising disappointment and resignation as acceptance and satisfaction. This was a cruel distrust. His father didn't deserve it. His father stayed up late, drinking beer and flossing his teeth and watching soccer on TV by himself. His father spoke four languages plus some Russian and he'd read every story J.F. Powers ever wrote, but life, it seemed, was a chore he was just trying to get through in good spirits.

Ed knew this was the wrong way to think about life but he didn't know the right way, so he called his sister back, thinking maybe she'd unwittingly offer him a clue. She didn't answer but there was no reason to leave her a message: he knew she'd call him as soon as she saw his missed call. She loved him, Ed knew. It felt good to know this. And maybe this was the clue: love feels good and should be pursued. If this was a clue, it indicated nothing about what he should do.

He took another hit from his one-hitter and sunlight came in through the small window near the ceiling and he thought about how the afternoon is so inviting when you aren't inside it. So he remained there, in his room, all afternoon.

4

Around nine on Wednesday night, one of his friends, a thirty-year-old woman, texted him: "everyone's going to the union. not that anyone cares if you come." She portrayed herself as someone who pretended she cared about nothing in order to hide her embarrassing sincerity. These were layers of self-consciousness that weren't worth unraveling; at the core, there existed something as false and insubstantial as a Facebook profile. He barely liked her, but he'd spent the afternoon trying to write a short story based on an anecdote his mother had told him about how one of his sister's friend's sisters had contracted cat scratch fever from her now ex-husband's pet falcon. The story was clever but empty and he was tired of trying to think about how to solve this problem, if you could even call it one—a problem—so he went. He rode his bike.

His bike was a mountain bike. It had been his brother's. His brother was six years younger than him and was getting a Ph.D. in physics. It was a nice bike, even though it was built for a fifteen-year-old six years ago. It was too small for him. He would be thirty in the near future and he was riding a bike that didn't have a seat because he'd gotten drunk one night and had left the bike outside a bar and had gotten a ride home and had forgotten about the bike until he was back at the bar a few nights later and went outside to smoke a cigarette even though he'd quit and noticed a bike that didn't have a seat. It had looked so different decapitated this way that it took him a few seconds to realize that the bike was his. He went from being amused to being annoyed. He went from being annoyed to being indifferent. He left his bike there for two more weeks, until he felt, as he often felt, that he was fucking everything up and that he needed to act responsibly and so made a list of manageable things that he should do. *Get bike* was on the list and so he walked downtown and got it. He rode it home and put it in his garage with a broken lawnmower and a lot of scrap lumber and left it there all winter and started riding it again in the spring and now it was June and he still hadn't replaced the seat.

Ed locked the bike up outside the Union Hall, which was only crowded on weekend nights, when country cover bands played for no cover and people came to dance. It was a Wednesday and a ping-pong table was set up on the dance floor. Men sat at the bar. His friends sat at two tables pushed together. He decided to get a drink before he went over to say hello. He did this to establish that he wasn't all that excited to see them, that he was more excited to drink cheap Canadian beer than to see them. He was an exceptionally deliberate person. This precluded him from enjoying life, as he was always trying to use his life to accomplish some useless end, such as demonstrating superiority to people he was ostensibly close to.

When he had his beer, he went over to the table and noticed Taylor there. She looked at him with a combination of dismay and pleasure. She sat beside a chubby guy who Ed had never seen. Who was of course her boyfriend and who lightly put his hand on her shoulder to show that, yes, he was. There used to be mall punks and now there were mall hipsters and the boyfriend was one of them. The boyfriend wore a new flannel shirt and had a slightly interesting haircut.

Someone said, "What's up?" and Ed answered, "Not much," as he always did, and someone else said, "This is Taylor."

"Hi, again," he said, and gave her a little wave. She was striking but calm, with a coyness that seemed to disguise self-assurance.

No one introduced the boyfriend, and Ed went to the only open seat, as far away from Taylor as possible, which was a relief. He'd need to drink a few drinks before he could ignore the boyfriend and make himself seem charming to her, which he wanted to do, even if it were pointless.

Ed drank and talked to the people he sat beside. He sat beside an overweight twenty-two-year-old poet from Missouri and across from the friend who'd texted him and across from his roommate, who was drinking what looked to be rum and Coke. They talked about a television show common to their childhoods. This was typical of their conversation—shallow, clever, and part of an attempt to demonstrate the humility of their intelligence via engagement with popular culture.

Though he looked down on everyone's self-awareness, Ed acknowledged that it was impossible to avoid completely— and he acknowledged that he hadn't avoided it completely. But at least he was aware that self-awareness, both in fiction and in life, acts like an echo chamber: it creates a false depth. At least he did his best to combat his self-awareness by opening himself to the possibility of sincerity, to the risk of sentimentality.

Ed wanted to be loved, to be in love. He tried to make the people he was talking to laugh so he'd seem funny and popular and he looked over at Taylor intently but rarely, so that she would feel he was interested in her but doubt that he was. In this way, he aimed to maximize her attraction to him.

Ed got drunk and so did everyone else and so they went elsewhere, to the Golden Rose, where they always went. When Taylor's boyfriend was talking to a few first years beside the digital jukebox and Taylor was standing alone at the bar, waiting to order a drink, Ed approached her.

"How's it going?"

It was a question too broad to be answered well. It was a mistake.

"Fine." She laughed. "How are you?"

"I'm good. Great."

It was awkward, but he resolved to wait it out. On the TV above the bar, cowboys walked slowly toward the camera, down the aisle of a train car. The bartender came and took their orders. Ed ordered whiskey, to seem tough and interesting. Taylor ordered water.

"Water?" he said.

"I have to wake up early."

"Oh, yeah? Why?"

She looked shy. "I have to take my boyfriend to the airport. His flight's at like six."

"Where's he going?"

"Home. California. San Diego. He wants to move out here, but he can't quit his job."

"Why not?"

"He's an accountant. I don't know. I guess it's hard to find jobs here?"

"Guess so."

They watched the TV together, waited for their drinks. When they came, she said, "See ya."

Her loveliness was someone else's—some California accountant's—but he wanted it, whatever it took. He wanted her to be his. He remembered her on Mount Jumbo and across the Union Hall and standing beside him just now, and he tried to stay cautious. Desire, he reminded himself, is how the world tricks you into disappointment.

He turned, leaned back on the bar, and watched Taylor feed a dollar into the jukebox, scroll through endless options, dance alone to a country song he didn't recognize. He listened to the lyrics: *I've got a table for two way in the back, / Where I sit alone and think of losing you.* When her boyfriend came to get her, she followed him out, obediently. When she got to the door, she looked back and made eye contact. Blond and calm and lit from behind by the pink neon light that lined the inside of the bar's windows, she looked angelic, like she'd swooped in to solve everything forever.

5

On a Sunday afternoon, Ed's friend Dave texted him and invited him to go swimming at a swimming-hole hot-springs combination called Nimrod. Ed had never been but he'd driven past it. Anyone who'd ever driven through Montana on I-90 had. Nimrod was right next to the interstate. Within ten yards of the paved shoulder. He texted back to accept. When Dave texted to tell him he was out front, Ed walked through the living room in his swimsuit, carrying a towel, and said, "See ya," to his roommate and left out the front door.

Dave, like everyone else Ed knew in town, was in the graduate writing program. Dave wrote semi-autobiographical short stories about being confused in Central America and converting to Mormonism for a high school girlfriend. That kind of thing. Dave was smart and gregarious, and Dave smoked cigarettes.

"You're looking at the pack like it's making you hungry," Dave said. "Just take one if you want."

Ed was constantly trying and failing to quit and it was a beautiful day and the sun felt like you could reach up and reach it, so he accepted. The cigarette tasted terrible until the last drag and then he wanted another and knew he'd be hooked again, would have to quit again.

Dave told him a few other people they knew were already there, at Nimrod, but Ed didn't ask who, because it was always the same people, all of them enrolled in the writing program. They ranged from cool to fine to painful. It would be whoever it was. There was no point in knowing.

They drove along a river, through huge, smooth mountains. They drove thirty-three miles east of town and saw a line of cars parked on the other side of the interstate. They turned around at the next exit and parked on the shoulder, at the front of the line. Then they walked between the wall of cars and a mountain that rose up steeply on the other side of them. They walked through tall grass littered with garbage. A guardrail replaced the wall of cars. A semi passed fast and made a burst of breeze that relieved him. It was hot. Ed stared at an approaching girl who was wearing a knee-length tie-dyed T-shirt and had an eyebrow piercing. They made eye contact and she said, "Fuck you, Harry Potter," as she passed, and Ed felt dumb and ashamed for being out of place and for judging those who belonged.

Up ahead, he saw a shirtless person jump off a rock, kick through the air, and disappear. He couldn't see the water yet but it was down there, somewhere between where all the people stood on the rock, awaiting their turn to jump, and I-90.

Girls wore bikinis and girls smoked cigarillos and boys had tattoos and small children were in tears and there was a waterfall from a beer commercial and the stale smell of sulfur hanging low and heavy in the air. They put their stuff down and took off their shirts and Ed had been able to forget about his tumor but now he saw it and remembered and now he'd have to begin forgetting again. It was like his cycle of smoking. He wondered if he'd die. He watched two fifteen-year-olds make out eagerly, suggestively, groping all over. He watched Dave walk down a creek bed into the water, which wasn't a pond. It was a small body of standing water beside a highway. Dirty-looking people were crowded into it.

Ed watched Dave swim toward the heads of their friends and didn't think he wanted to go in but then he saw that one of the heads was the new girl's. It was Taylor. He couldn't stay out now. He'd look like an idiot.

He walked carefully down the creek. The bottom was sharp. He made it to the water. It smelled rotten. It was sulfur from the hot spring that fed this hole. He waded in. It was tepid. He swam over to where his friends and Taylor were and Taylor said, "How's it going?"

"We're swimming in a ditch," Ed said.

Taylor laughed and so did everyone else. They talked about how weird this was. It was a common topic of conversation, the weirdness of things.

Every time he looked at Taylor, she was looking up at the mountains rising up behind him, like she'd just looked away to avoid him, to appear contemplative and appreciative. It worked. He wanted her attention. He asked her if she'd ever been to Montana before she moved here. She told him that her dad was from Butte and that her family had a cabin on a lake maybe ninety miles from where they were swimming and that she'd spent every summer there and that her grandparents and an aunt and her cousins all lived in various places around the state. She asked him where he was from and he told her South Carolina and she said, "The South." She said it wistfully. "Is it like all the country songs say?"

"Exactly like all of them," he said.

"Well, good," she said. "I hate being lied to."

They soaked in the ditch with dozens of trashy tweens and teens and talked about where they'd gone to college and about the town where they now lived and about the writing program they were both in and he tried to seem relaxed but he was nervous to impress her and she seemed both eager for everything to happen immediately and assured that all of it would. She told him about places in Montana she'd been with her family and wanted to return to, places he imagined as pristine and majestic, and he thought about how they'd all go back to town and get drunk after this and about how lovely she'd be and about how they'd hold hands under a table while she told him how boring her boyfriend was, how badly she wanted to break up with him. She made him romantic.

There was a yellow rope hooked to a rock near them, and Dave said if you held it and followed where it went, you would swim under a rock and surface in an enclosed cave. One by one, his friends went under with their hands around the rope and disappeared and returned with conflicting descriptions of a small, dark space. Ed didn't want to do it but he wanted to impress Taylor, so he held the rope and swam beneath the surface but didn't follow it to the cave. He just held his breath as long as he could, surfaced, and said, "It was just like I expected."

He suspected that he hadn't been gone long enough, that no one believed him, but no one said anything. Then only Taylor hadn't done it.

"Come on," he said.

So then she went under. When she returned to the surface, she said she'd hit her head and asked if her head was bleeding.

"No," everyone said.

Then she turned and all of her blond hair was tainted red. They gasped. She was bleeding pretty badly. She looked at Ed pleadingly, and he couldn't decide what he was supposed to do. Her eyes filled with tears and she swam off, back to shore, and a couple of girls followed after her and he didn't. He didn't want to intrude.

He felt embarrassed and bad that he'd urged her to do it. In the end, though, it all turned out fine. The other girls wrapped her head in a towel and dried her hair and Taylor's head stopped bleeding and they took her home. Once they were all safely gone, Ed and Dave got out of the ditch and stood underneath a waterfall of fresh water to clean themselves. As they drove home, it seemed like such an important incident and also like nothing had happened.

6

Targets made from cutouts of cute animals—a sloth, a kitten, a baby panda—were set up in Hal's and Allison's backyard. Hal was a poet from Wyoming. Allison was his gutter punk girlfriend. They'd lived together the year before in a minivan. Now they lived together in a studio apartment on the first floor of a big house with a small backyard of dead grass. They were having a party. There were thirteen people there, eleven of them graduate students in creative writing, all of them drunk at 10:15 on a late summer night that still wasn't quite completely dark. It was light enough still to see the targets, to aim an air gun at a cutout of a panda and pull the trigger and have a chance of hitting it. The rule was, if you hit more targets than your opponent, you got to take one shot at your opponent's back, which you'd feel and wouldn't like but which wouldn't exactly hurt.

Ed competed against Taylor. She beat him, and he pretended he'd allowed it.

"Turn around," she said. "And put your hands on your head."

He stood there, tense, anticipating the pain, and when the bullet came, he flinched but that was all. "I hardly felt it," he said, turning around. She held the gun like a child playing an adventurer. "But it was a good shot."

Then she took on the next challenger, a male poet wearing a flannel shirt, and Ed watched, jealous, with a tall boy
of Rainier. The male poet beat her and shot her and Taylor
screamed and Ed wished he were the male poet.

Ed went inside and sat on a futon, beside a punk girl with
a shaved head who he'd never met before. She wasn't a poet
or a fiction writer or a nonfiction writer.

"What do you do?" he asked her.

"Nothing. I work at Noon's." Noon's was a chain of convenience stores. "The one over by"—she pointed in the direction
of the university campus—"wherever."

They talked about Noon's and she told him about being
held up at what she thought was gunpoint but later found
out was just a toy and then Taylor came in and saw them
and Ed saw that she looked hurt and he was relieved to see
that she was jealous of him, too. To exploit the feeling and
increase Taylor's desire, he talked to the punk girl for a little
longer. Then he went to get another beer and to find Taylor,
to take advantage of her doubt.

He found her outside, talking to Jade, a nonfiction writer
who'd become Taylor's closest friend in Missoula and in
the writing program. Jade was Taylor's age, had grown up
in a Buddhist community in the southwest, had worked
as an assistant to a Mexican soap opera star in Phoenix
for a while after college, and had been published three
times on the blogs of prominent national magazines, a
credential that made most of the other students in the
students' writing program highly jealous. Ed didn't like
Jade, though not for her online publications. He didn't
like her because she was at once eager to please and aloof,
cutting but petty. He went over to her and to Taylor. He

had an extra beer and when he got there he held it out for Taylor.

"I got you this."

"But it isn't even my birthday."

Jade asked Ed how he was and he answered vaguely and Jade saw someone else she wanted to say hi to, so she left. She left them there alone. They stood next to each other, in silence for a second, and it was exciting, just standing there. It felt like something important was happening, like they were becoming a couple. Like her response to him talking to the punk girl and Jade's sudden departure from their conversation weren't coincidences. Like she'd finally begun to respond to his intense interest, which he'd been trying to express as subtly as possible, in order to limit the effect of failure, for the past eight days, ever since she'd cut her head at Nimrod, during which time he'd gone out every single night, hoping to see her and to see if he could get her to express an interest in him. An interest in being with him, instead of her boyfriend.

He'd gone to the Golden Rose and the Union Club and Al's & Vic's and the Rhino and the Top Hat to meet up with varying groups of writing students, nervous each time both that she'd be there and that she wouldn't be. When she'd been there and he'd seen her across a bar, holding a beer, he'd felt what he could only call *joy*, since that's what it felt like, and sometimes she'd catch him and sometimes she'd look back at him with what looked like delight, and every time she did so, it was exciting and a relief. But mostly she didn't. Mostly she hadn't even been there and mostly she'd avoided him when she had been there and sometimes, with a frequency that seemed to indicate intent, Jade or one of the other girls she'd begun to be friends with would clumsily remind him in conversation that Taylor had a boyfriend. And the night before, even though he was tired and it was rainy, he'd gone with some people to sit outside the minor league baseball stadium where Bob Dylan was playing a concert, in order to listen in without paying for a ticket. He'd only gone in the hope that she might be there, but she wasn't and they could barely hear anything except some distorted blues guitar from where they were sitting, in some wet dirt behind where the stage was set up.

The few times during those eight days when he had talked to her, Ed had been nervous and awkward and they'd only exchanged information. She'd told him that she was five years younger than him, had graduated a year before from a party school in San Diego, was 5' 5", liked Mexican food, had written Harry Potter fan fiction on online message boards as a tween—but none of that mattered. She made information arbitrary. He didn't know her but he knew already that she didn't think the way he did, grinding through options and doubts and anxieties before arriving at every inconsequential decision. She unspooled feeling, let herself go wherever she felt herself unraveling.

"I guess I don't really know," she said, for example, when he asked her why she'd applied to the writing program in Missoula. "I just wanted to be somewhere new."

He wanted to follow after her. He suspected it would lead him to love. He knew it was corny and that he should be cautious but she was infectious and, standing there in the backyard, it felt like a feeling was accumulating between them. Maybe he was wrong, but that's how it felt. It felt like the feeling would burst as soon as they touched.

They didn't touch. They watched people shoot air guns and drank beer.

She said, "My uncle Rick, he literally shot himself in the foot once," and they both laughed and she told him a long story, set in Butte, in what sounded like the '70s, that involved her dad, her uncle, and these two Indian guys who picked them up when they were trying to hitchhike to a lake—Green Lake—to go fishing. The story was elaborate and pointless, like a work of art. But before she could finish it, before she even got to the part where her uncle accidently shot himself, when her dad and her dad's brother were in a Dillon, Montana, mall parking lot, in the backseat of a car they believed the two Indians owned, when this old guy with a pistol tucked into the front of his jeans had just accused them of stealing the car and had ordered them to get out, which they refused to do, a thirty-one year old fiction writer from Oregon interrupted her to say "What's up, Taylor?"

"Oh, hi."

A painfully pointless and stilted conversation ensued. He waited for it to end, so she could finish her story, but then Jade returned and then everyone went to the Golden Rose, where, when she and he and everyone else was drunk, she finally did tell him the ending.

"Yeah, so my dad and my uncle Rick, they're like sitting in the back of this car and these guys come up and they're like, *You stole this fucking car. This is my car*, one of them says." It seemed like something he remembered happening in a movie. A movie about a writer who can't finish his novel. "And they're arguing and my dad's trying to explain that it's not their car and that they're just waiting on these other guys who they don't know. These two Indian guys who are in the mall for some reason. And not even they know why they're in there. And, anyway, the old guy's just like, *I don't care, get out of my car*, and all this stuff. And the whole time he's just got his hand like this"—she put her hand on her waist—"to hold his jacket open and show them that he's got a gun tucked into his pants. His jeans or whatever. So my uncle Rick, who's kind of this super annoying guy who lives in Oklahoma now—he finally just reaches out the window and grabs the guy's gun." She looked at Ed wide-eyed, to acknowledge his amazement. "I know, so then of course the guy reaches in to try to get the gun back and my uncle Rick just accidently pulled the trigger. Shot himself in the foot."

They both laughed. It was still funny, the second time.

"So then," she said, "he's just, like, gushing blood in the back of this car. And the old guy's worried about the car— since it's his and everything—and so he's trying to pull my uncle out of the car and my dad's trying to help my uncle and then, of course, the Indians come back and they see my dad and my uncle like fighting with this old guy. And anyway, my dad ended up with the gun and he got the old guy to back off and then the Indians—they took them to the lake. Green Lake. To go fishing."

"But what about your uncle's foot? He just went fishing with a bullet in his foot?"

"I don't know. I guess so." She laughed. "I guess that's the boring part, so no one remembers. Or I don't anyway. Or I do, but that's no way to end the story, with a trip to a hospital for a minor emergency."

"No," he said. "It's not. Don't change a thing."

7

E d went with Dave to meet some friends at the Western Montana Fair. He only went because he knew Taylor would be there. And there she was, wearing cut-off shorts and a red tank top, with a purse slung over her shoulder, watching someone dirt bike dangerously around a mesh metal orb. He stood beside her. He no longer felt nervous around her, he realized. He felt assured of her interest. She smelled like shampoo and brightened when she noticed him and said, "Oh, hey."

"How's it going?" he said.

"Nervous," she said. The person on the dirt bike was zooming along the horizontal axis of the orb. "I guess that's a twelve-year-old boy. He's named Roberto or something."

Roberto slowed down and settled on the bottom and removed his helmet and revealed that he was, in fact, a Hispanic child. Roberto waved to the crowd, which cheered. Ed clapped. So did Taylor.

"It's a whole family," she said. "A dad and his sons."

"That's amazing," he said and he meant it, though he didn't know quite what it meant.

Roberto was replaced by Henry, who was sixteen and who worked his way up to looping the orb along the vertical axis. He wondered if the act bypassed impossibly high insurance

premiums by only hiring employees who were related to
the owner, since even if a son died, the dad would only have
himself to blame and sue.

Just as he felt himself becoming jaded and less impressed,
Roberto was reintroduced to the orb and Henry remained
inside and they started up their bikes and began riding on
intersecting courses. Only their timing prevented them from
colliding. It was hard to imagine a less efficient safety mechan-
ism than time. They rode at top speed, missed each other by
milliseconds. Taylor looked away and said, "This is awful."

Ed realized his mouth was hanging open, so he closed it.

Afterward, he, Taylor, Dave, and Jefferson, a former army
medic and current poetry student with a soul patch and
prematurely graying hair, walked in the direction of a slowly
swaying pirate ship and reminisced about their terror and
amazement and Jefferson referred to the orb as The Ball of
Death, and the term reminded Ed of his tumor, which had
incubated and grown inside his body and still grew inside
it and sometimes sent a twinge of pain down his arm, into
his hand. That was all he knew about the tumor. He knew
he should Google "cancer" and try to find out more, but he'd
once heard on TV that fatigue was a symptom and then didn't
sleep for two weeks. It wasn't the kind of problem you can
solve, so he chose not to treat it as a problem. He chose not
to treat it at all.

He followed when everyone agreed to seek out funnel cake.
They found it and ate it. Someone bought ground beef mixed
into a bag of Doritos and sold as Taco in a Bag for $2.50. They
went around to the rides and some of them went on them
but Ed and Taylor never did. Instead, they talked and she
told him about when she used to be an evangelical Christian.

"Until when?"

"I don't know," she said. "I mean, maybe I still am."

He laughed. He stopped himself when she didn't.

"I mean, I still believe," she said. "I just don't know what I believe."

The pirate ship swung above them and the riders screamed and he said, "I hear you."

He'd been raised Catholic and still occasionally went to mass—but only when things were going poorly and he wanted to be in the company of other people also trying to make sense of the insensible. Not that they succeeded. They failed too but they didn't stop trying. It was comforting, but he didn't see what it had to do with God. It was much more mundane than that, than Him. Taylor seemed to be describing something else, a suspicion of her own limits, not of God's.

She talked about mystery and beauty. She was excited by the incomprehensibility of these topics but wary of simplifying them. She said, "I just can't believe I'm here. It makes me feel so lucky and confused."

She was something other than self-aware. She was full of doubt and belief and generosity and desire. She was excited, exciting. She made him feel he could be, too. So, though he'd told her that he hated rides, which made him only sick and scared—neither of which he wanted to be, obviously—he got in line for the Zipper and leaned against the seat in the tight cage that he shared with a Canadian nonfiction student named Jessica and that was made of a metal mesh like that of The Ball of Death. When the machine started up, the cage rocked and swung and rose above the gaudy lights of the fair and turned upside-down and hung there and the change fell out of his pocket and he clasped onto his keys and phone and worried about his glasses and was scrunched and nervous and tried not to press against Jessica's large breasts and he wanted to scream and so he screamed and he felt sick and scared but so what? He wasn't Roberto or Henry. He wouldn't die—and neither would they. Not for a while, anyway. He'd be released and Taylor would be there and then something else would happen.

And it did: a group of eight of them went to a bar and everyone got drunk and a subset of them decided they'd go sneak into the outdoor hot tub of a riverfront hotel. As they went, the world was shaky and dark and hard to follow, like he was watching it on some poorly recorded home video. There were streetlights and headlights and houses and pavement and the voices of their friends ahead and he lagged behind them, with her, and they didn't say much to each other because there wasn't much to say. It was time to do something but he was too nervous to act. She walked close to him and he wanted to take her hand but instead he just let his hand bump and brush up against hers and gave her the chance to take his. When she did, he felt a bounding, boundless feeling. It was something like joy, relief, and release all at once, except it couldn't quite be any of those because he'd experienced all of those and never this.

They passed under a leafy tree that swished coolly and he stopped and pulled her closer and they kissed and lust and love were the same thing.

"Come on," she said and he went with her.

They walked hand-in-hand and stopped a few times to kiss and climbed over the stucco wall that hid the hot tub and their friends were already there, stripped down, swimming, and soaking. They decided not to go in all the way, to just take off their shoes and socks and sit on the edge of the hot tub with their legs dangling in. They were establishing already the private world where they would live together for the rest of their lives. Or so he imagined then, as they sat together, touching for the first time.

When a hotel employee came to kick them out, he invited her over. She walked home with him and they made out in his green room, on his queen-size bed. It was as intense as a fist fight. They pressed and pushed into one another like they wanted to take everything out of each other and keep it for themselves. She stopped him and breathed heavily and was flushed red and she said, "I have something... I need to tell you something. I'm a virgin. I'm sorry, it's—"

He stopped her and assured her. "I don't care," he said. "It's fine," he said. "It's good."

"It is?"

His idea of her innocence had not only been confirmed but surpassed. He loved that he would have her all to himself when he had her. And maybe he already did. Maybe she was his. He said, "It's good," then kissed her more gently than before. "I don't want to sleep with you anyway." She laughed. "Your boyfriend would get mad."

"Boyfriend? What boyfriend?"

"I thought you had a boyfriend."

"I did."

"Till when?"

"Till yesterday."

"You broke up with him?"

"I wanted to be free."

"Well now look at you."

They both laughed: they were lying beside each other, facing each other, holding on to each other. They slept like that, fully clothed, for four hours. Then she kissed him goodbye and went home. It was barely dawn.

8

Taylor was from a planned city that had failed totally. A sociology professor had designed it in the '50s with only a set of vaguely utopian ideas about urbanism to guide him. He'd bought a huge plot of worthless land in the Mojave Desert and paved an enormous grid of streets and put a park at the center and put a fake lake at the center of the park, and he'd even helicoptered in a bucket of water from New York's Central Park to begin filling it. This, he claimed, was a symbolic gesture: the torch of urbanism was being passed. But the torch couldn't be lit. The torch was a bucket of water.

Only a tiny fraction of the land was ever sold. Various minor celebrities, including Erik Estrada, the then-star of the show *CHiPs*, had been enlisted for advertisements but nothing could convince a critical mass of people they should move to an empty, isolated, sprawling, sandy town with little opportunity for employment, so she'd grown up in the only house on her street, which was a cul-de-sac, a little capillary of civilization dying in the desert.

Her dad was a mining engineer at the largest open-pit mine in America. Her mom was a dental hygienist. Her brother still lived with them and delivered pizzas. Her friends from there were all charismatic Christians and she had an endless amount of strange stories about them. About dead people being given gold teeth by God and about the crimes of foster siblings and about innocent people in jail for killing their kids and about dating her pastor in high school. She wanted to write a novel about all of it but she didn't know how she could do it without exploiting all the tragedy she'd somehow evaded.

"But did you?" he said.

"Yeah. I mean, I'm here."

They were sitting on a pack bridge, above a creek that was tumbling down a canyon, three miles from a trailhead that was an hour's drive from Missoula, and she was telling him that she'd been briefly married to the accountant she'd just broken up with.

"It was only for a few days," she said, "a few years ago, not long after we first started dating."

The bridge was complicated and new. The wood was brightly varnished and the bolts were clean and everything was suspended on thick gray-black cables and she kept calling the guy he thought of as her ex-boyfriend her "first husband," even though he was the only husband she'd ever had and even though he hadn't been her husband in so long.

Ed didn't want to know about the marriage but she told him that she'd dated John—her ex-boyfriend's name was John—for a few years in high school and then they'd gone to college together and when they were freshmen John had asked her dad for permission to marry her and her dad had said it was up to her and John had proposed on a beach and she'd accepted, she said, to avoid embarrassing him. So they drove up to Reno but they didn't tell anyone, not even her dad, what they were planning to do and they were wed by a woman in a white suit but afterward she couldn't sleep with John in the expensive hotel room he'd rented for the weekend because, she said, she felt like she was being tricked into it and on that Monday morning they got it all annulled by a nice judge. She seemed to want to allow this to be information without the elaboration of meaning.

"But I don't understand why you married him, then."

"I know it sounds crazy, but I think I thought I was pregnant. I mean, I was a virgin but I'd just convinced myself or something. And still," she said, looking down at the water that rushed underneath them, "I know it's impossible, but still I sometimes wonder if I was. If I was but the child was taken away from me. But I don't like the idea of whoever would've taken something like that away."

He became acutely aware that he had no idea who she was. This awareness alarmed him. Who was she? Not who he'd imagined. She couldn't be. His imagination didn't extend that far, into her. It was too tangled up inside himself. Maybe she could show him the way to escape. It was that hope, he saw, that had led him to her, to here.

"But then we stayed together after that," she said. "Just dating. I guess I felt guilty. But it was never the same. It was going to end. And finally it did."

A dog ran up the bridge and arrived at them. They were sitting with their legs over the edge of the bridge, with a wooden support separating them. The dog was at face level and panting. They petted it. Ed scratched under its collar. Taylor rubbed under its ear. The dog ran off, back down the bridge. Back to its owners, he guessed.

"It's not important," she said.

"No," he said.

Sometimes he wanted to understand everything better. Sometimes he doubted there was anything to discover.

9

He wanted to impress her, so he rented a decommissioned fire lookout from the Forest Service for one Friday night and invited her to come.

"From the pictures online," he said, "it looks like it's on top of a mountain."

They drove a half hour west on the interstate, got off at the exit for a town called Superior, passed a house with a hand-painted sign out front that read PHIL DIRT WANT, laughed a lot about it, and followed printed-out directions down a series of numbered dirt roads to a gate with a combination lock. He'd been given the combination when he rented the lookout. He unlocked it and they continued on. Around the next corner stood what looked like an air traffic control tower.

They parked beside it and climbed a narrow stairwell that wound up and through the cinder-block base. At the top was a small, square room with huge windows. The windows reached from a few feet above the floor to the ceiling and wrapped all the way around, except at the corners. In one corner was a sink and a stove with one range. In another was a desk with a topographic map of the observable landscape. Another corner had a La-Z-Boy, strangely. Another had a twin bed in a metal frame. A balcony made of metal grating wrapped around the outside. It made no sense, this elaborate tower out here, ostensibly meant for monitoring fire activity but seemingly built in the era of more sophisticated methods for doing so, such as by airplane or satellite. It seemed to him like a front, a red herring, a means of concealing an abandoned missile silo or something.

They grilled and drank a few beers and went to bed early. There was nothing else to do.

"I'm sorry," he said.

"Why?"

"I thought it would be fun."

"Come here."

She was lying on the twin bed, on top of a sleeping bag, wearing a white tank top and pink gym shorts. He lay beside her and she kneeled over him, pulled her hair back into a hair tie, leaned down and kissed him, moved her ass against his lap, his hard dick. He felt her nipples under her shirt, made them hard. He felt her panties, which were already wet.

"Don't," she said.

He touched her and she tried to remove his hand but he took her arms, pushed her over, onto her back, put his hand inside her underwear, and kissed her until she began to shake, as if giving up and letting herself collapse, coming hard, pushing up against him, begging him to stop. When he did, she turned away.

"What did you do to me?"

"I want you."

"I know. But you have to wait for what I want."

When she fell asleep, Ed got up, went to the La-Z-Boy, and masturbated to the idea of what could've happened. Then he returned to the bed and slept deeply, dreaming of fire, and awoke not long after dawn, with her sleeping against him. He lay there for a long time, unmoving, even as his tumor shocked his arm and birds flew on the other side of the windows and trees moved in the breeze.

When she awoke, they decided not to stay the second night he'd booked, to find somewhere suited less to contemplation and more to "adventure," as she called it. Though unsure about quite what she meant, he agreed.

He drove and she surfed the radio until she arrived on the right song. The right song was always a corny, over-produced country song from the past twenty years. She looked out the window, alert and content, silently singing along to a song about July Fourth. She liked this kind of music purely. It was the music her parents listened to, the music she'd listened to for her whole life. Listening to pop country was something she did without wondering whether she should. He'd never done anything like that. Maybe, he thought, making her happy could be like that.

They drove on a two-lane road that ran along a pristine river and through lush late-fall mountains. In a town called Paradise, they stopped at a thrift store and tried to find something worthwhile from the past of this place. She found a sweater and he found a radio, but they didn't need either, so they didn't buy either. They went back out into the afternoon and saw a train roaring right past them, twenty yards away, on the other side of the parking lot. It clattered loudly, like it might fall apart right in front of them. Then the last car—a backwards engine instead of a caboose—revealed a standard main street—bars, boarded-up storefronts, a vacuum cleaner repair shop, a post office—backed with the swell of beige mountains that led back to where there was nothing they'd ever see. He imagined meadows, sunlight, silence.

She said, "I'm having fun."

They got back into his dented sedan and kept driving. There were more mountains and rivers and small towns with a bar and a post office and not much else. There were mountain goats grazing on the side of the highway and he told her about an article he'd read a year or so before in the local newspaper about a man who plowed through an entire herd outside of Anaconda and killed four trophy rams and almost a dozen ewes.

"My grandpa knew that guy," she said.

She seemed too involved with coincidence, too close to where everything connected, if such a place exists. He felt like she was taking him there, like he was entering a new life. His only fear was that he'd lug his old one into it. His old one was cautious and soft. His new girlfriend—that's what she was, wasn't she?—was not.

"They were on a board together," she said. "The water board at the lake where my grandparents live. The guy said the sun was in his eyes but my grandpa said he was drunk."

They stopped at a scenic turnout and looked. It was scenic: mountains, a river, clouds moving as slow as ships. They kissed. They turned at a Forest Service sign and drove up a dirt road and walked through a silent grove of huge cedars. They stopped at a roadside bar and had a beer in the late afternoon. They pulled into a gas station in a tiny town and asked the attendant if there was a hotel nearby and she said, "You're at one."

Then she led them across the parking lot to a low strip of motel rooms. She carried a single key on an oversized neon key ring and showed them what they could have for $49.95. It looked exactly like a motel room. His girlfriend—that's what she was, he decided—said, "We'll take it," and the attendant said, "It's all yours."

Ed followed the attendant back to the convenience store to pay. When he returned, Taylor was curled up on top of the slick comforter and he came behind her and she flipped her hair up so he could hold her comfortably. Her love was generous. He fell asleep with her and awoke with her. Then they went to find something to eat.

They passed a closed senior center that doubled as a coffee shop. They passed a closed video store. They passed a storefront with a name plaque that read MAYOR and was screwed into a closed white door. They passed houses and cars that could have been anywhere but were here and were therefore strange and interesting and beautiful in the dusk plus occasional streetlight. They walked down a dirt alley and dodged puddles and were barked at. They walked maybe five blocks and came to what seemed to be the end of the world. Train tracks marked the boundary. Behind the tracks, there were mountains and forests so impenetrable they seemed empty, so empty they seemed hollow. It wasn't the end of the world. It was the end of Troy, Montana. Canada was over there somewhere, if you went far enough.

A bar stood across the street from the tracks. The bar was wooden and had a little covered patio on the side. A Buick LeSabre and a scooter were parked out front. A sign said Home Bar and she said they might have food there and he said, "Let's see."

Inside, it looked like a bar. There were pool tables and taps and a smudged mirror obscured by liquor bottles and a few tired people sitting on stools and poster-size beer advertise-ments on the walls and an analogue jukebox. The bartender, a thin woman with hairsprayed hair, waved hey to them as they sat down. Here, Ed decided, everything was only what it seemed. It was like church in this way. He knew that he was just a tourist taking in the authenticity of poverty but he tried not to think about that now: the whole point of being here was to avoid awareness. He ordered a whiskey on the rocks when the bartender came over.

"Well OK?"

He always ordered well whiskey but now it felt like using a credit card in a thrift store: evidence that he was trying to be poor, choosing to be. Still, Ed said, "Sure."

Taylor ordered a Jack and ginger and the bartender looked displeased, like she didn't approve. They asked about food and ordered the only item on the menu: a frozen pizza cooked in an oven designed especially for it. They ate it. He burned the roof of his mouth. Out the windows, the sun sank behind the mountains. A clock advertising Black Velvet said it was 9:36. They ordered new drinks, the same ones. He noticed a sign made with notebook paper and magic marker taped to the mirror behind the bar: "Smoke and I'll light you on fire." A few more people came in. Ed went to the bathroom and the walls were covered with pictures of nude women from back issues of *Playboy*, women whose hair had to date them (to the mid-'90s, mostly), since they couldn't rely on their clothes to do it. When he came out, his girlfriend was talking to an unnaturally thin middle-aged woman.

"This is Wanda," Taylor said.

"How's it going?" He reached out to shake her hand and hers was as fragile as a bird.

"Your lady said you guys like doing karaoke," said Wanda. "Said you do a good 'Margaritaville.'"

He couldn't tell if she was making fun of him. "I don't like to brag."

"Hey!" Wanda yelled out to the bartender and the bartender looked fake annoyed, like they had some mock-antagonistic rapport between them. Then the bartender came over and Wanda said, "Hey, listen, we got these two folks in from Missoula and they want to do some karaoke. What do you say?"

The bartender was reluctant but Wanda persisted.

"I mean, why not?" the bartender said, in the end.

It had always seemed to him like a desperate reason to do something. Now it didn't. It seemed like the only reason.

Wanda walked off, triumphant, and the bartender brought them more drinks. Then they played pool. Then they spent a half hour on the eight ball. Then he scratched. Then Wanda walked over and slapped Taylor's ass and Taylor laughed and Wanda winked at him and Ed did nothing. Then Wanda went outside and he watched her smoking through a window that held a neon Miller Lite light.

Ed got drunk and so did Taylor and then Wanda was on the bar's high stage, welcoming everyone to karaoke night at the Home Bar. There were some cheers and a few guffaws and Wanda sang "Pretty Woman" poorly, like she was reading the words to the melody instead of anticipating and singing them. Meanwhile, Ed and Taylor flipped through pages of plastic sleeves containing songs alphabetized by title instead of artist. Taylor pointed to ones she might sing and he didn't recognize any of them. She wrote the requisite information on a scrap of paper and gave it to Wanda when Wanda was ordering another drink at the bar and a cowboy was singing a Moby song.

Lots happened. Taylor sang a song called "Strawberry Wine" and she looked like a country star, even if she didn't sound like one. An elderly man did a heartfelt rendition of "God Bless America" and got a standing ovation. Ed got drunk enough to sing "Luckenbach, Texas" and everyone was too drunk to listen. A man who called himself Hoss asked Ed with old-fashioned politeness ("Excuse me, sir," etc.) if he could dance with Ed's girlfriend, and Ed allowed it and felt powerful giving permission and was turned on and watched his pretty young girlfriend dance with a handsome man wearing a cowboy hat. Watching, he wanted her to be his and knew she was and realized he was on the brink of being too drunk to have sex and knew that he could sleep with her now because now she was his, so he said, "Let's go," when she returned to the table and they did.

As they went back through the town's empty streets, they held hands and laughed. When they arrived, they kissed and were quiet in the bed's cheap and cold sheets. The world was somewhere else and they were here, in a gas station motel room. He did his best to be gentle but she gave herself and her generosity made him want to take. He felt the warmth of her blood and he said, "It's OK, baby, it's OK," and she said, "Be careful, be gentle." Then they slept and he held on to her, as though otherwise she might flee.

10

They went out to eat and they went to bars. They sat in inner tubes and floated down a river with their friends and a laundry bag full of beer cans. They went on bike rides and walks and hikes. They talked about everything, told all their best stories. They spent a lot of time in each other's bedrooms, making out, talking, laughing, and sleeping, often in the middle of the day, exhausted by each other and indifferent to everything else. They made love as quietly as they could, so their respective roommates wouldn't hear. They made love but she wasn't on birth control and it always seemed awkward to stop and put on a condom and it didn't feel as good when one was on and she didn't insist, so they rarely used protection and only when sober. They hoped for the best and they worried afterward and he consoled her, assured her, told her he'd take care of her if she were pregnant.

"Which you're not."

They were talking on the phone. He was lying on his bed, in his bedroom. She was lying on her bed, in her bedroom. It was late September, and they'd been a couple for five weeks. He was hungover and had smoked his one hitter but he couldn't get the headache he'd had all day to fade away.

"No," she said. "I really think I am."

"Why? I mean, didn't you just have your period? We haven't even had sex since then, have we?"

"I know, I know. It's just... I look pregnant. I have, like, a pregnant belly."

"No you don't." He laughed, despite being frightened. Or because he was. "Remember the last time this happened? With John or whatever?"

"No," she said. "This is different. Let me come over. I'll show you."

Ten minutes later, she knocked at his front door. He opened it. She turned to show him her profile, lifted her sweater, and revealed her round stomach.

"You're pretending," he said. "You're pushing your stomach out on purpose."

He laughed and so did she. Their laughter expressed their disbelief.

"I know it's not possible," she said. "But I clearly look pregnant, don't I?"

"You do."

"It's crazy."

"Let's name her Cindy," he said.

"No," she said. "No!" She was laughing but she wasn't happy. "That'll make it real. A name will."

"I'm sorry," he said. "It's just, this is weird." He thought again of her first false pregnancy, but he said nothing. He couldn't let this become evidence of some flaw in her, some insanity. He had to indulge her, trust her. He had to show her that it wasn't real, because it couldn't be. "What do you want to do?"

He took her to the student health center. He waited in the waiting room, read a magazine article about how the Internet alienates us from ourselves and each other. She came back sheepish. They'd prescribed over-the-counter laxatives.

"They asked me if I wanted to see a 'mental health professional.' Talk to someone."

He hugged her.

"Don't think I'm crazy."

"I don't."

"Or dumb."

"I know."

"It's just, I'm not afraid of anything, when it comes to us."

11

Her family owned a cabin on a lake. The lake was a couple hours east of Missoula, in the mountains, far from anywhere except Anaconda, a dilapidated mining town. Her family had bought the land on the lake fifteen years before and had bought a used mobile home and placed it there. For the first few years, Taylor and her brother and her parents and her aunts and uncles and cousins and grandparents had gone to the cabin occasionally, for holidays or for long weekends or for weeks at a time during the summer. They'd piled in there. They'd slept on floors, on love seats, in sleeping bags. Or so Taylor told him, recalling it all so fondly, telling him long stories about driving four-wheelers with her grandpa and about her parents getting into enormous fights and about a second cousin's wife who committed suicide there for reasons that were unclear.

Eventually, though, her dad and her Uncle Toby and her grandpa had decided to add on to the trailer. They'd built a porch. Then they'd built a little two-room cabin with a finished basement on the other side of the porch, so everyone could have a little more room. And so on until they'd built by hand a two-story cabin with a full, finished basement and a wrap-around deck and six bedrooms and two bathrooms. But they'd built this larger structure around the mobile home, so that one house was trapped inside the other, larger one. They'd kept the mobile home there, Taylor explained, because it contained the kitchen, which would be the hardest and most expensive thing to build themselves.

But now, Taylor told Ed, they'd decided they were ready to replace it, so her dad was coming up to Montana to work on tearing the trailer out of the cabin.

"I'm gonna go down, and see him. Do you want to come?"

Did he? Did he want to meet her dad? They'd only been dating for two months, but he did. He did because he loved her, he knew, and because the cabin sounded interesting and because it would be fun to get out of town with her.

So on a gray late-November Saturday, they drove down a scenic highway and turned onto a dirt road that looped around a large lake that held the reflected image of the gray-and-white mountains standing on the other side. Ed drove her vehicle, a cheap SUV. She told him where to go, directed him to the driveway. He parked before the cabin, which had a high, peaked roof and had glass installed in the entire front. The glass faced the lake and the mountains. Besides the glass, the rest was logs and rough-hewn wood.

"It's crazy that your dad built this. It's like a nineteenth-century McMansion."

They went inside. The heads of elk and deer looked into the living room, and a huge grizzly bearskin hung on one wall but the stretched fur was too large for the wall, so its left paw clung to the ceiling.

"My grandpa shot that," Taylor said. "My other grandpa. The Alaska one. It was a record grizzly for a while."

How had he arrived here? He followed her from the living room into the kitchen.

"This must be the famous trailer."

It was a seamless transition, though it was apparent when they arrived—when they were standing below the low ceiling, on the rotten linoleum, within walls of warped wood paneling, before an ancient, stained range—that they'd left the spare and rustic construction of the cabin and arrived somewhere else, somewhere worse. They went through a doorway, into the mobile home's dining room and there, at a table with a vase full of fake sunflowers as a centerpiece, sat a middle-aged man bristling with the clean-cut strength of a high-school football coach, an elderly man wearing suspenders designed to look like a carpenter's ruler, and an elderly woman with a perm and wearing a red Christmas sweater. They were all drinking cans of Miller Lite, and they all exclaimed when they saw Taylor and they all stood up to hug her and shake his hand.

"It's beautiful here," Ed said.

Taylor's dad nodded and said to his daughter, "So, do you want to see what we're doing?"

He opened a closed door and Taylor followed him and Ed followed Taylor and they stepped into a small hallway. They walked down the hallway and arrived in a bedroom with one of its exterior walls almost entirely gone. What remained of them was splintered wood. Otherwise, they'd been replaced by the outside. Outside, it was cold and it was dense with brown-and-green pine trees. Inside, there was shaggy brown carpeting and them.

"So you're finally doing it," Taylor said. "Getting rid of it."

"No turning back now. We're gonna do this bedroom and the bathroom next door this weekend. Then we'll do the dining room and the kitchen next summer. We've gotta dismantle every stick of this thing, eventually. Then we've got to decide what to do with all this space. And then of course we've got to do it. Put in a new kitchen and a dining room and maybe a master bedroom right here. So it's gonna be a long process."

"It's amazing," Ed said.

"I wouldn't quite say that," Taylor's dad said. "It's really kind of a piece of shit."

Taylor laughed and so did Ed, less easily.

"It hardly even needs us," her dad said. "It's returning to the earth already." Then he opened a closet door and said, "See," and Ed saw several large mushrooms growing up from the brown carpet. "And just think," Taylor's dad said to his daughter, "your grandparents were living in here until yesterday."

He closed the door and Taylor asked him if they could help.

"Well, sure. You want to take down that wall?" He pointed to the wall that separated this room from whatever was on the other side of it.

"How?" she said.

There was a sledgehammer and several kinds of crowbars scattered across the floor.

"However you want," her dad said. "It doesn't matter. You can't mess up."

"OK."

"I'll grab my beer," her dad said, "then I'll come back and help. You guys want one?"

It was 10 a.m. but Ed couldn't say no, so he didn't. "Sure," he said, and so did Taylor, and when her dad was gone, Ed picked up the sledgehammer, looked at Taylor, and said, "Here goes."

Ed heaved it up and put a hole in the wall. And another and another. And the hole revealed what was on the other side: a group of five boys, all on bikes, stopped in the thick woods, marveling at what was happening: a house was being slowly, violently demolished. A house within a house. And he was the one demolishing it. Who was he to do this? He did it, swinging the hammer hard and quickly developing huge blisters on his thumbs. It felt productive, tearing something down.

That night, they slept together in a twin bed, in the loft that overhung the living room where the bear skin was pinned and the animal heads were mounted. It was extremely hot and dry up there, due to her grandfather's constant feeding and stoking of the wood stove, even in the middle of the night, at seemingly regular intervals. He slept uneasily and when the sun came up, he looked out the huge window, out at the lake, which reflected and multiplied the dawn light, and the idea that her father was in the house, that he was taking his daughter, turned Ed on, so he touched her until at last she responded, turning to him to kiss him, her mouth stale with sleep.

They made love quietly and when they were done, they lay there hot in the heat and he draped his arm over her and she picked it up to remove it and when she did, she looked at the lump on his arm and looked frightened and said, "What's that?"

He was no longer alone, he knew, and he knew now that he always had been. He didn't know what to say. "I don't know," he said.

She turned on a lamp and they looked at it.

"How long's it been there?"

"I don't know." He didn't know it yet, but this would become his refrain, his mantra, a form of assurance as everything became ever more incomprehensible. "A year?" He could think of no reason not to downplay his irrespon-sibility. "Less?"

"Have you talked to a doctor?"

"Not yet. I just—"

"But it's..." She looked lost in feeling. "Can I feel it?"

He looked at it and saw it and saw that it was a tumor, that solipsism might actually kill him, that this would be a fitting end for someone so self-involved. "Why not?" he said.

She barely ran her finger over his hill of skin. "Does that hurt?" she asked.

"No," he said. "It's fine. It only hurts once in a while." Maybe he could justify his failure to take care of it. "Just barely, like a little twinge or something in my arm. It's OK."

"Yeah but it's pretty big."

"I can see that."

"Please, will you go to a doctor?"

"Well it's probably too late now," he said, feeling cruel and sorry for himself. She turned away from him. He climbed over her and spoke into her face: "I was kidding," he said.

"Well I'm not," she said and didn't turn back over. "I love you," she said without looking at him.

He looked out the huge window, at the mountains and the lake and the sunlight and he wished he was out there somewhere, but he was here, alone with her. "I love you, too."

12

He barely noticed the tumor, except when he lay in bed to sleep or when he awoke in the middle of the night due to the persistent pain or when Taylor brought it up, which she often did, in an attempt to get him to make an appointment to see a doctor, which he kept putting off doing until one morning, when he awoke to pain ceaselessly shooting down his arm, into his hand, like the tumor was spreading something into his system. Some kind of poison.

So that morning, with the pain only escalating, he called the main number for a clinic housed in the hospital and tried to explain the tumor to a nurse, who advised him to make an appointment with a dermatologist, which seemed ridiculous to him but which he did, since a pointless appointment was a way both to do something and also to further delay his diagnosis. When your body begins to attack you, it's difficult not to feel disassociated. The distance between your consciousness and whatever else you are feels vast. Life looks far away, out of your control.

The appointment was in two days but he decided to lie and tell Taylor it was in four days, because he wasn't yet ready to let her unimpeded into his life. Or actually "not yet" wasn't quite right: he had been but now he wasn't. He'd allowed her in and now he had a tumor instead of something to avoid confronting and now he wanted to go back to filtering his life before it arrived at her. He wanted her to know what he wanted her to know about him. He wanted to love her on his own terms, though he knew this was the wrong way to love.

So Ed went to his appointment alone, and the dermatologist was alarmed by the tumor and confused about why Ed had come to her. She ordered him to see an orthopedic surgeon as soon as possible, and she arranged an appointment for later that same day. Between appointments, he went to a bar.

The bartender said, "This one's on me."

"Why?"

"Don't ask that," the bartender said. "Just take it. I'm trying to help."

"OK. A whiskey."

"Hey," a regular said from the far end of the bar. "How about me? You never give me shit for free."

They all laughed and Ed raised his glass and the regular came and sat beside him.

"I had three different moms," the man said. "Three. You know that meter maid who drives around downtown in the little golf-car thing? She was the third one. The nicest one. The other two, they were mean. Just terrible."

"I'm sorry."

"I'm just saying," the man said. "Don't be in here feeling sorry for yourself." He laughed cruelly. "Just look at me."

Ed drank his drink in one drink and left. He'd only been inside for a five minutes, but outside he was surprised to see the sunlight, to find it was still day. It was like coming out of a movie matinee. As the whiskey soaked into this brain, the alcohol increased the distance between his brain and his body, which made it easier for him to see the orthopedic surgeon, to accept the surgeon's alarm about the tumor and how long it had been there, and to agree to go down to the hospital's basement for an MRI.

He descended a newly painted white stairwell and got lost in a maze of linoleum-floored hallways and came to the right door and went in and spoke to the attendant and filled out paperwork for the third time that day and read a back issue of *Newsweek*, which he was surprised to discover was still in print.

Then an elderly man holding a clipboard called his name, and Ed was brought into another room and asked a series of questions—Do you have any pins, plates, or pacemakers? Are you claustrophobic? Height? Weight? Birth date?—and given a gown, which made him think of his sister folding hospital laundry on the other side of the country, outside of their hometown, in a facility near a swamp that had recently been deemed a national park. Then a female technician with braces showed him into a sterile room that contained only the huge tube of an MRI machine. He lay on the tray, as instructed, and the nurse asked him if he wanted headphones, so he could listen to the radio while he was inside the machine.

"I don't know," he said.

"You should," she said. "Otherwise, you might forget you're alive."

She smiled when she said this, like it was a reference to something he should know about, so he took them and asked her to put on sports talk radio. She said she would and instructed him to be very still, otherwise they might have to start over.

He put the headphones on and thought, *I'll just pretend like I'm an astronaut going into outer space.* Then the tray retracted and the voices of former athletes came into his head. They were in the middle of a conversation about whether or not a relief pitcher who'd recently blown his elbow would make the Hall of Fame. The voices—histrionically opinionated and insidiously ingratiating—demanded that he listen. As he listened, their words led back to the mouths that made them and the mouths were holes in faces that were on heads that were on strong bodies that were in rooms with foam-covered microphones and cluttered desks and fluorescent lights and boxy computer monitors. He saw the callers in their wood-paneled kitchens, on their rotary telephones, at Formica tables strewn with opened junk mail. It was somehow nine years or so ago in his imagination: everyone smoked cigarettes inside, unrepentantly. He wanted one.

Meanwhile—while he collapsed inside himself, assumed paralysis, felt himself calcify, fossilize, become dysfunctional—the machine made whirring noises that sounded like a robot seeing and made hammering noises that sounded like a nail gun being aimed at him. Then there were occasional moments when machine and radio silences coincided, when he felt the world retracting, when he felt maybe like an astronaut tethered to but drifting away from a space station. It was terrifying. Then, after forty minutes, the tray he lay on retracted and he pushed himself up and turned to let his feet reach the floor but he couldn't feel it: both of his legs were dead.

13

Two days later, she came over to take him to the appointment he'd had two days before. She rang the doorbell and wore a dress. She looked beautiful and worried, like a wife. They got in her car and she drove and she asked him what was the matter and he tried to explain that the initial appointment was actually on Tuesday but that there was another appointment today.

"I had the MRI already, but today the surgeon's gonna tell me what the tumor was, I think, which is actually more important, so it's really kind of better to come to this one, since the other one was just me lying in a machine for an hour, doing nothing, and this one... They might tell me something."

"Sure," she said.

"What?" He knew how he'd offended her but wanted her to say it.

"You don't always have to convince me of something," she said.

It wasn't what he'd expected her to say. "I'm just telling you the truth," he said. "I'm trying to be honest."

The orthopedic surgeon's office was in an annex of the town's secondary hospital, which was from whatever school of architecture came up with those low, spread-out public schools with covered outdoor walkways. It was aggressively utilitarian. There weren't even windows, except at the ends of the long hallways. They waited in the waiting room. The magazines were either about cars or houses, were for men or for women. They were called back and waited in a fluorescent-lit exam room.

"Let me see your glasses," Taylor said, "and let's see if they make us read the eye chart the same way, like if my eyes with them are as bad as your eyes without them."

She was wearing his glasses and reading the chart when the surgeon came in. She gave him back his glasses and tried to explain: "We were testing our eyes. Sorry."

He put his glasses on and everything came into focus.

"This is my girlfriend," he told the doctor.

The doctor said hello and proceeded: "I consulted with the radiologist about your MRI and the good news is, the tumor in your arm looks benign. It's a very regular-shaped tumor—sort of like an egg shape, so we think it's probably something called a 'schwannoma,' which are rare but, as I said, benign. Which of course is good."

"So," Taylor said, "it's not cancer or something."

"No," the doctor said. "That's right. We don't think so. It's highly unlikely."

"Not cancer," Taylor said. "Just wanted to be sure."

Ed had spent so long cultivating an abstracted attitude about the tumor that it was difficult to feel relief. Instead, he felt validated: he had a tumor but he wouldn't die. He'd been right to ignore it, even though he'd been wrong about why. All he said was "Weird."

Taylor reached over and took his hand.

"The thing is, though," the doctor said, "this isn't something I know much about, schwannomas. Very few people do. Few doctors. I've seen one or two of them, the tumors, but they're very rare. They grow in the nerve. I think you'd be better off if you saw a specialist. Except there's only one specialist, and he's in Boston."

"But do I need surgery?" he said. "Have it removed?"

"That's a question for him. Dr. ..." The doctor flipped through his clipboard until he came to a name. "Kay. Dr. Kay. He's in Boston. I have a phone number."

"So he's OK," Taylor said. "He's fine."

"That's a difficult question. It depends what you mean— and without more expertise, more information, I don't think I can really answer that. It's not the kind of question that has an answer, as far as I know. But Dr. Kay, he'll have more information for you."

When the doctor dismissed them a few minutes later and they were walking down the long hall, toward the one window at the very end, which was bright with light like a train coming into a tunnel, she said, "So, how do you feel?"

"Like no one knows anything," he said, "especially not me."

14

After putting it off for a week, Ed called the doctor in Boston, who was a neurologist, which seemed strange to him, since nothing was wrong with his brain. At least not medically, he thought, making a dumb joke with himself. He talked to a secretary and left a message and then a nurse called him back and he tried to explain and she asked him when he could come in.

"For an appointment? In Boston?"

"The end of the month's the soonest we could see you. Say the 28th?"

"I live in Montana," Ed said. He said it like it just occurred to him.

"But you want to make an appointment, right?"

"I'd have to fly out there. It'll be expensive."

Not that money was an issue, obviously. He took his bike to the free bike shop, but a free bike shop was a charity for the affluent, for people who didn't need anything but liked the feeling of satisfying a need and so deprived themselves in small ways so that they could experience the gratification of desire. He was one of these people. He liked to read about communists and hardship but he only had to teach one section of one writing class a few hours a week. He could easily buy a ticket but wanted to make it seem difficult, even to a stranger, over the phone. He told the nurse he'd need to hold off, so he could get a cheaper flight. She scheduled his appointment for six weeks in the future. She asked for his address and said she'd send him a list of things he'd need to do before the appointment.

"What kinds of things?"

"Not much. A hearing test, an eye exam." She had a Boston accent so unreal it couldn't be real. "That kind of a thing."

After he hung up, Ed rode his bike to campus, which someone once told him had been built on an Indian burial ground. School had started again, and he was teaching fiction writing this semester instead of composition. He had no idea what he was doing.

He rode slowly. A crossing guard helped him cross a road, in front of an elementary school. On the elementary school playground, the children played, frenetically. He rode past a park where a male body builder jumped rope alone. He rode through a neighborhood. The houses here were simpler than elsewhere. The cars were older. The trees moved more easily in the breeze. The clouds were more physical, powerful. The sky didn't seem quite so far away.

He went to the building that contained the humanities departments and the classroom where he taught. He went up the stairwell, past a strange mural that contained numerous fetuses and seemed to be about the growth of knowledge and the universal value of learning. He went to the classroom, which was already full of students who'd rearranged the desks—chairs with little tables attached—to form a circle, as he'd asked them to do when they arrived before each class. The circular arrangement, he'd explained, helped facilitate discussion during workshop.

He sat down in a desk like all the others, except that, unlike all the others, his wasn't next to any others. There was a buffer between him and whichever students showed up last and had to sit nearest to him. He removed his notebook and his stack of the three student-written stories they were going to critique that day. One of the stories was a rape fantasy about a library worker, one was a story about knights and dragons that he didn't bother to follow, and one was a quirky Lorrie Moore-like tale of a self-conscious but hilarious young person. As he sat there in the few minutes before class started, he flipped through the stories, trying not to look at the pretty girls in the class and imagining that they were looking at him, desiring him.

After taking roll, he began to talk.

"Fiction," he said to the twenty-two college students who sat around him, looking at him, "is just a compelling lie." Then he asked them to write a paragraph about themselves that was not true. When they seemed wary, he said, "Look, I'll do it too."

He sat there but it quickly became clear, as he ran through things potentially worth writing about, that only the truth is worth recording, so he wrote nonsense in his notebook, so his students wouldn't know that he couldn't complete his own assignment.

15

It was February and weirdly warm and it rained and he walked across a rectangle of pavement labeled Physicians Parking Lot. This was the campus of Missoula's other hospital, but it looked more like a Bosnian community college that had been bombed in whatever that war was called. Entire buildings seemed to be missing; it was probably just bad planning. He was slightly hungover and he was going to an audiologist's office for a hearing test, per Dr. Kay's nurse's instructions. He was looking for Building Two. He asked the only other person around if that was Building Two.

"No, *that's* Building Two," the woman said, pointing at an identical building across a large parking lot.

He'd told Taylor about the appointment but he—or actually his parents, though he didn't tell her that—had bought her a ticket to accompany him to Boston and she'd already helped him a lot and this was just a hearing test, so he'd prefer just to go alone. He could tell his decision hurt her, but he pretended not to notice and now he wished she was with him. He always talked himself out of what he wanted.

He crossed the large parking lot, took an elevator, discovered Suite 300, opened a wooden door, and found fanned magazines and a woman with sleek sunglasses dangling from her neck. This was the outdoorswoman's version of a necklace. It seemed too casual a kind of jewelry for a doctor but, then again, she wasn't a doctor. She was an audiologist. Which is the kind of thing you have to have a certificate to do. Like fixing the plumbing in someone's house or grinding lenses for a person's glasses.

He noticed a rack of pamphlets about deafness. They talked. He could hear OK. He was here because he had a benign tumor and now a neurologist in Boston had ordered some tests, but he didn't know why the neurologist had ordered the tests.

"In other words," he said, "I don't know why I'm here."

"Well," the audiologist said, "sometimes benign tumors can be a sign of certain conditions that cause tumors to grow in the brain." She looked concerned. "But that's just a guess. I'm not a doctor. I don't know. I really can't say."

"But you just did."

The audiologist laughed and gave Ed a clipboard of paperwork to complete. The audiologist had feathered hair, expensive cowboy boots, boot-cut khakis, a fleece vest, and her sunglasses necklace. He imagined that when she made love she liked for the TV to be on in the background, so the kids couldn't hear, that she turned the TV to QVC, because it helped her relax. He filled out the paperwork.

Then the audiologist brought him into another room and instructed him to sit at a table, before a machine that looked like a child's idea of what a machine is like. It was gray and had maybe a dozen knobs and buttons and a little screen, like the ones on those computerized word processors that preceded computers. The audiologist told him that it would be like going up in a plane or into the mountains when she was pushing into his left ear what headphone manufacturers call buds. She was right: it felt that way. She told him all he had to do was relax. He listened to a series of high-pitched sounds and watched something get graphed on the machine's simple screen. He was a robot getting a tune-up. She moved the bud into the other ear and the same thing happened.

Then the audiologist took him into what looked from the outside like an out-of-place bank vault but turned out to be a soundproof chamber that contained a plastic chair, a battered Connect Four box, some stuffed animals, and various kinds of headphones hanging from hooks. He thought about what a child's jail cell might be like. The chair faced a window that opened onto another chamber that was the same, except that it just contained a computer on a desk. The audiologist selected a pair of headphones and gave him the kind of clicker he imagined contestants on *Jeopardy!* use to buzz in and answer. She told him to press the buzzer whenever he heard a sound. Then she disappeared. Then she reappeared through the window, in the other booth, behind the desk, at the computer. She put on a pair of her own headphones, then reached back to turn a dimmer switch down and faded away.

He listened hard for faint sounds and pressed the buzzer when he heard one. This went on for what felt like twenty minutes. He knew he wasn't doing well. His stomach was loud and difficult to hear over and he rarely pressed the buzzer. He believed that if he did poorly on these tests he would somehow be contributing to the growth of the tumors in his brain. He believed that he was doing poorly and dooming himself, and he wished he was just watching this on TV.

Then the test ended and the audiologist's voice came through the headphones to give him some simple instructions: "Just do what the voice tells you to do, OK?"

It seemed like something God would say. Then static started up in his left ear and an elderly man spoke in a very even tone into his right ear.

"Say the word 'hat,'" the man said and he said the word "hat."

"Say the word 'world,'" the man said and he said the word "world."

"Say the word 'tough.'"

"Say the word 'puff.'"

"Say the word 'lead.'"

"Say the word 'jar.'"

"Say the word 'huge.'"

"Say the word 'just.'"

"Say the word 'salt.'"

"Say the word 'cart.'"

He said the words and he wondered how the man who was talking on the hearing test got the job talking on a hearing test and he thought about how he should find a job that was meaningful, that would contribute something to the world, and he was distracted and he missed one of the words the man said and so he just said a random word—"kid"—and he felt like he was fucking up, like he was giving himself brain tumors. He hoped Taylor's children would never have to go through this kind of thing. They wouldn't deserve it. He tried to picture what their father would look like but he could only come up with an image of his own dad, a man who seemed underwhelmed by the world. Everyone said they looked alike. He tried to concentrate.

"Say the word 'well.'"

"Say the word 'heart.'"

"Say the word 'mouse.'"

"Say the word 'luck.'"

Then he took another test and another and then it was over and the audiologist came in and let him out of the booth and took him out of the office and onto the elevator and down to the ground floor and out of the building and across the parking lot and over to Building One and up another elevator and into a room in the pediatric wing of the hospital. It was the only room available. The walls and the ceiling were all painted the same white, a white that reminded him of teeth.

"Let me go get the equipment," she said and left him in the room alone, to look out the long window that looked down on a drab garden. It was misty out and the mountains were gauzed over with clouds and how could this be winter if this was the weather? He noticed an a/c unit the size of a mobile home on the roof of a lower building—Building Three maybe—and then the audiologist returned with a cart that held some complicated machine connected to a bulky Dell laptop.

The audiologist, who smelled like nothing, like she shower-ed without soap or shampoo and washed her clothes with just water, told him about this next test while she scrubbed his forehead and his earlobes hard with some abrasive cleanser and then taped one electrode just above his eyebrows and clipped the other electrodes to each of his ears. He was a machine connected to another machine and the audiologist instructed him to just lie down and relax and keep his eyes closed. So he did. He lay down on the pink comforter where so many children had lain and slept and been sick, holding their mothers' hands.

Though he wasn't wearing headphones, he started to hear a sound that sounded like a helicopter hovering nearby. He

wondered if the audiologist could hear it. Probably not. It
seemed to be amplified from inside his head. It was loud and
he thought about how beautiful Taylor must have looked in
her white dress, at her first wedding, holding the bouquet
of fake flowers that so many brides before her had held, that
was a prop owned by the casino that owned the chapel, and
he thought of dye dispersing in water and he tried not to
swallow, because he wasn't supposed to move and he hadn't
moved in so long that swallowing seemed as drastic as rolling over or sitting up. He thought, *Why be cautious? I should
move in with her.* The thought had to do with being afraid of
death, which all the medical apparatus reminded him was
imminent or at least inevitable.

When the sound finally stopped, the audiologist said
something like, "OK," and that meant it was over. He could
move. He opened his eyes, hatched out from behind his
eyelids. He sat up and noticed a flat-screen TV on a little
pedestal in the corner, near the ceiling. Beneath the blank
screen, attached to what you would call *the frame* if it were
a painting, there was a little fake bronze plaque that said, in
the font they use on soccer trophies, *In Loving Memory of
John Michael Lowell: 2003–2008.*

16

A girl wearing a pink "Virginity Rocks!" T-shirt leaned back in her seat and rested her feet on her mom's walker. An elderly Asian janitor named, according to his nametag, Chun, swept the carpet, wiped down the trash-cans. A voice on the PA system blamed the weather—rising heat, impending thunderstorms—for the weight restrictions on a flight to Idaho Falls. Men with goatees exuded false confidence. A black man with a Jerry curl honked the horn of a golf-cart-like intra-airport vehicle loaded with old ladies. An emo kid worked the fake Brooklyn deli across from gate B87.

Ed thought, *He is a person. She is a person. He is a person.* This thought was part of a larger effort to become accustomed to being in an airport, a place where no one belongs. He was here with Taylor but only until their next plane took them to Boston. She'd never been east of the Mississippi and was bummed that her streak was about to be broken.

"I've just always imagined it's more like what it's like to live on reality TV," she said. "*Jersey Shore* and stuff."

"It's exactly like that—crowded and bland. Like TV."

They sat side-by-side, facing floor-to-ceiling windows that showed an elaborate runway scene. He sat in his plastic chair and wished he'd become one of those people who guide jets with orange wands. He'd become a person who scurries around, trying to capitalize on his time alive. Taylor asked him what he was thinking about.

"That I'm grateful you're coming to this appointment with me."

She kissed him on the cheek. "It'll be fun."

When they boarded the plane, Taylor told him to take the window seat, which she'd been assigned. "Looking down reminds me that I'm in a metal tube, in the sky, which seems impossible and scares me."

The airplane was above a seamless ceiling of clouds for almost the entire flight. Then the captain came on and announced that they would begin their descent and Taylor closed her eyes and gripped the armrests and Ed turned his attention to the windows. He looked at the clouds, which were dark and thick and churned like bad water. He watched as the view was erased because they were inside the clouds. Inside the clouds, they were caught within an incandescent and undifferentiated white. It was the way movies represent heading toward the light of death and the airplane was stuck inside it. He kept expecting that the plane was now—now—now—now going to break through to the sky on the other side. To color and shape. To ocean and city. To green and blue and brown and rain and trees and buildings. But the white was pressing in on the window and on all of the windows and it pressed until he felt like the window might crack and come after him and he felt suffocated, claustrophobic, like he was in a tight white MRI tube.

"What's happening?" he whispered to her.

"What?" she said, her voice piqued with panic, her eyes shut tight and tightening. "What's going on?"

He looked at the white smothering the window and fantasized about smashing out of it, letting the air suck itself in and fill up the cabin and offer everyone cold, deep relief.

"Hey," she said. "Talk to me."

"It's OK," Ed said and as he said it the world slipped back into view, like a slide into a microscope slide holder. It looked schematic from so high up, but there it was: a thing composed of things, like everything. The world, it wasn't so special. "We're landing."

"Now?"

"No. Soon."

Everything got bigger as they got closer and then they were there and it was all the right size.

"It looks like an airport," she said when they were taxiing.

"See? It's not so different in the East."

They remained seated and held hands while everyone else scrambled to get their luggage from their overhead bins and jostled to cram into the narrow aisle and wait. They were the last ones off. The stewardesses wished them well.

17

He had an uncle who lived in Boston—or Cambridge, actually—and they were going to stay with him. They took the subway there. She'd never been on a subway. She kept losing her balance and laughing and he suspected she was pretending and flirting by falling into him and he was happy and he caught her and held her and she looked up at him and they told each other they loved each other.

Why did they keep telling each other this? It was the mantra that allowed them to ignore the world, which ignored them. He scanned the car for someone who was glaring at them, disapproving of their affection, but no one bothered. He scanned the car and he saw that everyone wasn't white and he missed Montana, where no one wasn't, and he felt indicted.

Ed had seen his uncle at least once a year, at his grand-father's Florida condo for Christmas, when he was growing up, but in the ten years since his grandfather died, he'd only seen his uncle twice. He didn't know much about his uncle. He knew that his uncle was his dad's older brother and that he was considered a genius and that he'd been married to two different women with the same name but spelled dif-ferently and that he'd divorced both of them and that he taught computer science at a community college and that he was an amateur mentalist and that his uncle's interest in mentalism had led to an obsession with trying to identity the pseudonymous author of a nineteenth-century book about card sharking that had become a foundational text for magicians. And according to Ed's dad, Ed's uncle had spent years working on a book about his quest to solve this mystery.

They got off the subway, and Ed rolled Taylor's rolling upright suitcase down the sidewalk. It contained both of their clothes. They got lost and he explained that Boston was a notoriously confusing city due to its haphazard layout and she went into an Au Bon Pain across the street from the brick wall of Harvard. A half hour later, they arrived at the inconspicuous high rise where his uncle lived. When they were trying to figure out the buzzer, Ed remembered being here in middle school with his family. His mom was sweating and holding his little brother. His sister was crying and sitting on the steps where he was now standing. His dad and uncle had gone somewhere. They were locked out.

Taylor pressed the buzzer and Ed heard his uncle's voice, reporting his name.

"Come up," his uncle said and they obeyed.

The elevator's carpet was unraveling. When the doors opened, they revealed his uncle. He looked like an old man, like a version of Ed's grandfather, who'd died a decade ago and whose last words were, "This should be interesting."

"You found me," his uncle said and they shook hands.

The hallway was narrow. Ed's uncle introduced himself to Taylor, crowded them, made Ed uncomfortable. His uncle started down the hall and they followed him into a surprisingly nice apartment. The wood of the floors was wide and old and the windows were large and clean. In the living room sat a handcrafted modernist coffee table, the kind you'd see in a book in an art museum gift shop.

"You can stay in the study," his uncle said and showed them to a small room.

There was an air mattress on the floor and a desk with a computer on it. The computer had a huge monitor.

"Great," they said. "Thanks."

"So you're both writers?" he said.

They reluctantly agreed, after providing numerous self-deprecating qualifications.

"So am I," his uncle said.

"Cool," Taylor said.

Then they all stood in the entryway to the study while his uncle told them about the book he was writing and about the pseudonym and about how possible candidates for the author's identity included a Peruvian diplomat, a St. Louis chiropractor, a Negro League outfielder's white widow, and a Texas saloonkeeper. Some even believed that Ambrose Bierce might've written the book, though that theory had been largely discredited.

Then he led them to the kitchen and began to make a dinner of pasta and salad. It was 4:30 in the afternoon. Ed wondered if his uncle was maybe insane but he knew it wasn't that simple. His uncle was governed by delusion but not of the kind that doctors can diagnose. Ed wondered if his failure to deal with his tumor had been a symptom of a shared condition and, if so, if his coming here to see the doctor was a sign that he was recovering from it.

His uncle began to talk about the publisher of his book and about some of the journals where he'd recently pub-lished related articles. Had he asked either of them a single question? Ed couldn't think of one. They ate dinner and the conversation moved to politics, a subject that neither of them knew or cared anything about, but Ed kept the conversation alive in order to keep his uncle talking, so they could just half listen and eat, which seemed like the easiest way to get through it. They were done eating at 5:15 and Ed told his uncle that they were supposed to meet up with a friend of his from college. His uncle seemed relieved, which seemed strange, since he'd seemed to be so excited to talk to them. In this way and in other ways, his uncle seemed to obscure himself so that he would seem inscrutable and therefore brilliant. His uncle gave Ed a spare key, and they went out. They went for a long walk. It snowed. They walked along the river. The wind blew. They discussed his uncle.

"That's not what I'm like," he said, "is it?"

"Aww," she said and kissed him like he was a kid and said, "Kinda."

He was like a kid: he could be easily assured. They went to a bar. There were lots of college students there and they probably went to Harvard and were smarter than him, even though they looked like frat boys and likely studied business and were even more privileged than him, and he and Taylor got drunk, mostly because they didn't want to go back to his uncle's house and couldn't think of anything else to do in Boston at night.

"We could ride the subway around?" he said.

"Why?"

He didn't have an answer. They went to a different bar. It was the same, except louder. It was somewhat fun. His uncle's apartment was dark when they got back.

18

I n the morning, they woke up late and whispered about being hungover and hoped his uncle was gone. Ed went out to check and found a note on the coffee table that read, in part, *Good luck at your appointment.* Ed realized he'd let himself forget about the appointment. The realization sent a shock through him, a shock of panic. The appointment was at 11:00 and it was just after 9:00, but Taylor always took forever to get ready and the subway might be delayed and the city really was confusing and he had no idea where they were going and he needed coffee and she'd want something to eat.

So Ed hurried her and they got in a fight and she accused him of taking her for granted and he accused her of not giving him the benefit of the doubt and they arrived at the appointment forty-five minutes early, without her cell phone (which she'd forgotten in the rush) and with distrust straining to separate them. He filled out paperwork and she watched him do it.

"Are you going to help me remember my last name or something?"

"Fuck you," she said and picked up the top magazine on the coffee table in front of them. It was called *Massachusetts Mom* and she pretended to read it, angrily.

"What? I was kidding. Jesus. Quit feeling sorry for yourself."

He knew he was right but didn't know that it didn't matter. They sat in silence until, ninety minutes later, a nurse called his name and showed them to an examination room that was like all the others, except with freshly painted walls and a thin computer mounted by a metal arm to the wall. It was as though the sterility of medical complexes was meant to bore you into being numbed into submission. *A kind of mental anesthesia*, he thought, thinking he was clever.

The doctor was a loud, short young man wearing a bow tie. The doctor was maybe seven years older than Ed was. No more than ten. The doctor spoke to them like he was dictating into a little digital recorder, like they were just receptacles for information. He told them he'd looked at Ed's MRIs and at his other records and that the tumor in his arm was, in fact, a schwannoma.

"Which is good," the doctor said, "because this means that, by definition, it's benign. However, the MRI also incidentally picked up a second, smaller tumor of the same kind in your sacral nerve, which is located in your lower back. Have you noticed anything there?" He hadn't. "Do you mind if I take a look?" He didn't. "Do you mind removing your shirt?"

He did so and felt the doctor's cold hands on his skin. They felt metal, mechanical. He felt a finger press against his collarbone, which he'd broken being born, and he felt a stinging soreness and flinched.

The doctor apologized and looked at the tumor in his arm and talked for a while before he said, "Because there are multiple tumors of this same type—schwannomas—it's highly likely that you have one of two extremely rare but closely related conditions: schwannomatosis or neurofibromatosis, both of which will cause these benign, egg-shaped tumors to grow in your body throughout your lifetime. The difference between them is simply that, in the case of neurofibroma-tosis, these tumors will grow not only in your body but also in your brain, which can lead to hearing and memory loss, among other neurological impairments."

Ed was sitting on the examination table and was uncom-fortable and adjusted himself and the tissue-paper sheet crinkled loudly. Taylor was sitting in a chair by the door, looking anxiously at the doctor, rapt with anxiety. The doctor leaned against a cabinet that probably contained cotton balls and needles, and he kept talking.

"Hence, the hearing test I had you take. The results of that came back, well, ambiguous. You do have some very slight loss in your left ear, but it's extremely minor and may be unrelated. Or it may not be. May not be unrelated." The doctor collected himself. "The hearing loss may be related."

"I did used to play drums some, in high school and college," he said, hoping to explain away his brain tumors. "Maybe that has something to do with it."

"Very possibly." It almost sounded like an oxymoron. "In order to know conclusively, however, I'm going to prescribe a scan of your brain, which will indicate the presence of any tumors. If any show up, then we will know that you have neurofibromatosis. If none appear in this scan, that's good but it doesn't necessarily mean we can conclusively diagnose you. Just because nothing appears in this MRI, that doesn't mean none will later." He looked at both of them. "Does that make sense?"

It was a cruel question.

"Well, then what?" Taylor said, speaking for the first time. "I mean, what do you do? Surgery or something? Take them out?"

"The short answer is no. There's nothing we can do, unfortunately." The doctor seemed like the kind of person who says please and thank you to his wife. "These tumors grow inside nerves, so surgery can be very risky. Any error at all, and you see a loss of function. And sometimes even if the surgery goes perfectly." The doctor talked to Taylor and Ed felt himself disappear from the room. "For example, if we excised the tumor in his arm, he could lose function in his hand, which of course would be very difficult to deal with."

"But what if it just keeps growing?"

"There are instances in which the risk of surgery is less than the risk of allowing the tumor to remain. For example, the tumor on the sacral nerve, in some cases, can grow large enough to cause difficulty in achieving and maintaining an erection and also causes issues with bladder function. But those instances are rare—and we can talk about those options then, if it comes to that."

Ed tried to decide if medicine's ineffectuality in this case was good news or bad. Not having surgery seemed like a good thing. Leaving tumors in his body to make him impotent and corrupt his brain did not.

"So but what if he has the thing where they're in his brain?"

"Well, it's difficult to say. As I said, he... you," the doctor said, looking at Ed, who looked away, at the ground, "will experience hearing and memory loss and perhaps additional depreciation of cognitive function, but there's no way to predict exactly. As I said, this is a very rare condition—only eighty-nine confirmed cases, internationally—so not a lot is known."

"But you'd just leave them?" Taylor asked. "Brain tumors?"

"We really don't have a choice. Surgery would do more damage than the tumors would."

"I'm sorry," Ed said, "but I'm confused: all I have now is a tumor in my arm, right? And my back, I guess."

"Exactly," the doctor said. "There's no reason to get ahead of ourselves."

Taylor didn't look relieved.

"Your parents," the doctor said, "do either of them have any similar tumors that you know of?"

"Not that I know of, no."

"I ask because this condition, it's genetic—at least as far as we know—so we'd expect one of your parents to have had these kinds of tumors. Schwannomas."

"Genetic?" Taylor said.

"A person has a fifty percent chance of passing it on to his children."

"A person?" Ed said.

"Unfortunately," the doctor said and though he kept talking and talking about risk and genetics and Ed's parents and nerve sheaths and his research and brain scans, it was the final word. Ed would have tumors for the rest of his life and he might go deaf and forget everything and so would his kids and so, therefore, would her kids, if they had kids together, and he suspected she wanted to and he wanted to give her whatever she wanted, unfortunately.

19

B ecause things had begun to go wrong, Ed drove to mass the Sunday morning after they got back from Boston. Taylor didn't go with him. She was more hungover than him, she explained when they were lying in bed together.

"Besides, isn't this a sin?"

He only went to mass when he wanted to find people who had enough faith to believe in an explanation. Mostly, though, he found a priest reading a sermon he'd found on the Internet to a small group of sad and earnest people who struggled to sing needlessly complicated hymns.

The church was a pentagon and the pews didn't have kneelers and the only windows were thin slits that ran along where the white ceiling met the white walls. It was everything wrong with innovation: its differences were superficial and arbitrary. Instead of lectionaries, college-aged kids handed everyone a few pages of Xeroxed hymns when they came in. The church band—teenage pianist, elderly trumpeter, female acoustic guitarist—practiced quietly before the service started. The priest wore a microphone on his collar and announced his own entrance to the ten or so attendees. During the processional, they sang a song with the lyric *We are the youth / Our future's a mystery* and Ed felt that maybe he might get something out of this. He could do nothing without considering its value.

The third reading was from Matthew and it began, "Therefore stay alert, because you do not know the day or the hour."

The priest was reading from an ornate Bible that he'd held up for everyone to see before he opened it. The priest was the only man he'd ever seen who had a goatee that made him seem sweet.

"For it is like a man going on a journey," Father Whoever read aloud, "who summoned his slaves and entrusted his property to them. To one he gave five talents, to another two, and to another one, each according to his ability."

Ed thought of Marx and Engels, who he'd claimed as personal heroes in high school, and he wondered if the priest had said "talents" or "talons" and worried that maybe he really was going deaf, that tumors were indeed swelling in his brain, deadening sound and whatever else entered his head.

"Then he went on his journey," the priest said.

Ed wondered where the man was going, but the priest didn't say. As the priest continued to read, it became clear he'd said "talents" and that talents were an ancient unit of currency and that this was a parable about money. The servant with five talents invests his money and doubles it. So does the man who got two. The man who received one, however, goes off and digs a hole in the ground and hides the money. When their master returns, he discovers what they've done. He's pleased with the first two and promises to reward them. The third man, though, comes to his master and says, "Sir, I knew that you were a hard man, harvesting where you did not sow, and gathering where you did not scatter seed, so I was afraid, and I went and hid your talent in the ground. See, you have what is yours." This infuriates the master, who calls him an "evil and lazy slave" and rebukes him for not at least putting the money in a bank and earning interest and takes the talent from him and gives it to the one who started out with five and turned it into ten.

"For the one who has will be given more," the priest read, "and he will have more than enough. But the one who does not have, even what he has will be taken from him. And throw that worthless slave into the outer darkness, where there will be weeping and gnashing of teeth."

When he came to the parable's end, the priest said, "This is the Gospel of the Lord," and everyone, including Ed, responded, "Praise to You Lord Jesus Christ," and Ed felt like he was agreeing to something he didn't understand. Christ, reputedly the first communist, couldn't possibly endorse the idea that those who have deserve more and that those who have not deserve nothing. And yet, the parable had ended before the right message had been conveyed, before the master's injustice had been punished and before the man with one talent had been rewarded at least with salvation, if nothing else.

The priest closed the book and put his hands together in prayer and bowed and then he began his homily.

"In today's reading from the Gospel of Matthew," he said, "we are offered a story about the rewards of stewardship."

The priest declared that one talent during the time of Christ was worth approximately three million dollars in today's money, and he explained that we can think of the talents in the parable not as literal currency but as skills and, well, *talents* that each of us has been given by God and that it is our duty to share them with others. The man with one talent was punished, the priest said, because he hid himself away from the world rather than making an effort to utilize what he'd been given. We, the priest said, should be like the men who invested their talents. We, he said, should be stewards of Christ. We should, he said, help the homeless, for example. Then he outlined three simple, practical ways of doing so: by donating to a certain Catholic charity, by volunteering at the local shelter, and by offering to work in the church's soup kitchen.

Ed allowed himself to accept the priest's interpretation and remained at mass and took communion and knelt down to pray for his lonely uncle and his retarded sister and his own brain but in the days afterward, he became certain that they'd all been deceived, even the priest. (Even the three-million-dollar calculation seemed flawed.) The story of the talents was a parable about greed, Ed decided, and the men who'd multiplied their money had, in fact, been punished: they'd become further indebted to their master, whereas the man who was a slave and who'd dug a hole and attempted humility was expelled but was therefore freed. Liberated.

Ed tried to find confirmation for this theory online. He found nothing but remained convinced. His conviction had to do with his own guilt, which had to do with the $82,000 he had and kept secret, even from Taylor.

20

During a blizzard, they went to a party at the apartment of a twenty-three-year-old fiction writer named Erin. Taylor had workshop with Erin but didn't know her well, despite having read a number of Erin's short stories, all of which were about aging fast-food employees who lived in their parents' basements. Erin didn't seem like the kind of person who would ever work in a fast food restaurant or live with her parents after high school. Erin had large breasts and black hair and would've been pretty if she hadn't behaved as though everything were a burden. It wasn't.

Erin's apartment was brightly lit and decorated with a menagerie of hyper-realistic looking stuffed animals positioned around the living room: a fawn, a border collie, a poodle, a white cat, a toucan, a turtle. One of the fiction writer's roommates was an environmental studies grad student and the other was a ceramics grad student, and all three seemed like equally likely candidates for the stuffed animals' owner.

Dave, wearing a souvenir sweatshirt from a Mexican restaurant in his New Mexico hometown, walked over, gave Ed a wry high five, and said, "What's going on, man?"

While they each drank a beer, they had a long conversation about the blizzard and about Roberto Bolaño, in which they speculated about the source of his greatness.

"It's that it always seems like he's lying to you but for no reason," Ed said.

"Why would he need a reason?" Dave said.

They went to the fridge and took expensive local beers brought by other people. When they returned to the living room, Owen, a former college pitcher whose favorite writer was James Purdy and who wrote accordingly, approached and asked them what was going on and they both said not much and, after an awkward pause that ended with them all laughing to acknowledge and dissipate the awkwardness, Owen told them that he'd brought a joint and did they want to smoke with him? They did. Owen had slept with Erin once and went to ask her if it was OK for them to get high and she said it was fine but that they should do it in the basement. They went and stood around a furnace, a water heater, and a huge stack of broken-down boxes.

"Well, this sure makes me feel like a deviant," Owen said.

"Yeah," Ed said. "It's almost like we're doing something."

Before they'd finished the joint, which included a rolled-up scrap of a business card at the end, they were already talking about how high they were. When they went back upstairs, Ed talked to the people at the party, people who were suddenly more interesting than they'd ever been before, and he drank more slowly and he petted the stuffed deer and he looked across the room at Taylor and felt rich with love. Her love was his talent. He was burying it—keeping it all for himself, no matter what God would've wanted. She was standing in a group with a few other girls and he motioned toward the door, to invite her outside with him. She laughed and nodded and put one finger up to mean *in a second.*

He put on his coat and hat and gloves and stood on the front steps, watching a pick-up truck struggle down the street. The truck swerved and stalled and continued on.

Taylor came out and stood beside him and said, "What's going on?"

"Isn't this crazy?"

"It's so quiet."

Snow was stacked on the trees' branches, like the opposite of shadows. He was out there to feel alive and open, to embrace the harsh weather, to see it as an opportunity instead of something to escape. He believed it was something she would like—both the feeling and that he was feeling it—and he wanted to impress her.

"Look in the streetlight," he said.

There, you could see the snow come down as steady and repetitive as TV static. It was cold but not terribly so, and the snow was a distraction. As they watched the blizzard, people came out of the apartment, marveled at the weather, said goodbye, and trudged down the sidewalk, on their way home or to bars or to other parties. Meanwhile, Ed and Taylor talked and Taylor told him about this one time when John, the guy she'd barely married, got mad at her while they were driving through the desert and just pulled over and left her there, beside the highway, fifty miles from home.

"Jesus," Ed said, high and happy to listen. "Why was he so mad?"

"I don't even remember. He was just always mad. He had this thing—this degenerative thing that was making him go blind, so he had to take steroids. They were supposed to, like, stop him from going blind. And they kind of worked—he could see but he got these big, thick glasses. Really nerdy but kind of cute. But the steroids also just made him mad all the time. He was just so angry. He'd yell at me constantly." She laughed. "He was so frustrated, it was scary."

"Yeah, but why'd he leave you in the desert?"

"He wanted to go to this car show in Bakersfield. Classic cars and stuff. He was really into that but he didn't even know about cars. Like this one time he bought this brand-new truck and drained the oil but realized he didn't have any new oil to put in it, so he tried to drive the truck to get more oil and totally ruined it. The truck was just, like, dead after that."

"It was?"

"Yeah. I mean, he was crazy." She paused, like she was recalling fondly his insanity. "I was just standing there, in the desert at night." It sounded like the Bible, like a lie. "My phone didn't work out there or anything, though, so I just started walking. So I'm walking down the road and then this car pulled up behind me and just scared the shit out of me, you know, so I started running. But then I heard him calling my name: "Taylor, Taylor." She whispered this part, the yelling. "I love you." And then he caught up with me and held me and I was trying to get away. Like fighting him and stuff but he was huge. He was in boot camp then and his waist was like this big"—she made a circle with her small hands—"and his shoulders were like this"—she pointed with each index finger to a place a couple feet from each of her ears. "And he literally carried me back to the car." She laughed. "It was crazy."

"This was before you married him?"

"I mean, we didn't really get married."

"He could've been your husband."

"He was," she said, smiling as though she knew what she was doing: making herself appear dangerous and strange. "Technically."

They sat there for a second in silence, thinking about the desert while watching a couple cross-country ski down the street, then decided to leave.

"I've just gotta grab my purse," she said. But when she went to the front door, she found it was locked. "What the fuck?"

The windows of the apartment were entirely dark.

"Are you serious?" he said. "We got locked out?"

She knocked. She cupped her hands and put her face against a dark window and saw that everyone was gone. She called every friend whose number she had and who'd been there, but no one answered and she left everyone more or less the same message: "Where'd you go? We got locked out of Erin's apartment and I left my purse inside. Call me back immediately. Bye!"

When she was done, she asked him what they should do and he suggested they just walk downtown, to the Golden Rose.

"There's a ninety-nine percent chance they're there any-way," he said.

They held hands and they walked, stepping high in the deep snow, which filled their shoes and soaked their socks. They walked down dark sidewalks and arrived at the river path. The river was the blank space between parallel stretches of land. Taylor's phone rang. Her ringtone sounded like a doorbell. It recalled simpler times. It was Erin. The back door, she told Taylor, was unlocked and they should just go in and get the purse and then come meet them, yes, at the Golden Rose, which was fun.

So they walked back and turned down the alley that he believed led to the back door of Erin's building but when they came to the back of the building, it was completely dark and he began to doubt if it was right, if it was actually Erin's building. It was three stories tall and he remembered it being only two. It had a wooden fire escape running up the middle, and he didn't recall seeing a fire escape when he went out back to bum a drag off one of Dave's cigarettes. They stood in the alley, looking at the building.

"I think this is it."

"You do?"

"Do you?"

Then she was walking toward the building, and he was following after her, afraid. Afraid he was wrong and that they would barge into the wrong apartment in the middle of the night, startle the tenants, and end up drunk and high and dealing with cops. "Hang on," he whispered as they were starting up the back steps. "Are you sure?"

"No," she whispered. "Not at all." She laughed.

She turned the back door knob and the door opened. She looked at him, put her index finger to her lips, and snuck in. Ed entered behind her, closed the door quietly, so it was just a click. It was dark, so he listened for her, heard her taking small steps. He imagined her moving Indian-style—heel-toe, heel-toe—and so he walked that way through what he knew was the kitchen by the hum of what must be the fridge.

She whispered, "Come on." She was close. His eyes adjusted and he saw the gleaming eyes of stuffed animals staring at him from the next room, the living room, and he knew that this was the right apartment, that they were safe, and somehow he knew that she knew too, that she was just pretending now, extending the thrill of potential danger, so he played along, was silent, stood still.

"Come here."

He went to her and put his hands around her waist, and she put her arms around his neck and kissed him, and they kissed there in the dark living room and she led him to the couch, which could be seen by the streetlight, and she sat on his lap and told him, softly, to take off her panties and he did and he pulled down his pants and he pressed her into the couch while he fucked her and he choked her while he fucked her and he called her a whore because it turned him on to do so and because he imagined, from the story she'd told him earlier about her first husband, that it turned her on too, to be controlled, and he kept his hand around her neck but didn't grip it tight and he came inside her and collapsed over her and she was silent and they both breathed heavily and he got off her, pulled up his pants, turned on the light, and saw that her face was red and slack and she looked like she was looking at something far away and gone. He said nothing. He would make her force him to apologize, if that's what she wanted him to do.

"My purse," she said.

He turned and saw that she'd been looking at her purse. He stood there and she pulled her underwear back on.

"We should go," he said.

They walked to the Golden Rose without talking, and the snow kept coming and coming.

When they arrived, she said, "You think you know what I want but you have no clue. You only think about what you want."

She went inside before he could ask her what he was wrong about, and they remained separated for the rest of the night.

When he woke up the next morning with a pounding headache and an overturned lamp beside his bed and Taylor still asleep beside him, the last thing he remembered about the night before was buying a five-dollar Pabst Blue Ribbon-and-Jameson combo that the bar called a PB&J.

He went to the kitchen to make coffee. While he waited for it to brew, he opened his laptop and read a story on the website of the local daily newspaper about an avalanche in a nearby neighborhood. It had leveled two two-story homes, temporarily buried three children, nearly killed a professor, and actually killed his wife.

21

He hadn't called his local neurologist and made an appointment to have the brain scan the specialist had prescribed and he wouldn't, because he didn't want to know what it would tell him. Even if it told him he didn't have tumors now, that wouldn't mean he wouldn't get them. And if it did tell him he had a tumor or tumors inside his head, there was nothing they could do anyway. The doctor had told them so. So what, then, was the point of knowing?

Taylor wasn't convinced there wasn't a point, but she felt sorry for Ed, she said, and overwhelmed by the situation, so she relented and agreed he was right. What else could they do?

"I just want you to know I'll stand by you," she said and he believed her.

They were on a dirt road, driving up into the mountains, when they crossed the state line. The sign that said Entering Idaho was riddled with bullet marks. Now they were in Idaho, which meant the trailhead was nearby. He drove her Jeep Liberty on a road slick and slushy with melted snow. Spring was turning into summer. She consulted a book of local day hikes and told him to turn at a certain Forest Service road. Then they parked in some tall grass and both had to pee and did so on opposite sides of the car, then started down an abandoned and overgrown logging road.

They were in the woods, the mountains, the wilderness, together, with a Nalgene and a bottle of bear spray. They were outmatched. The landscape was large and deep and impending. The trail was muddy with runoff. He listened and looked for bears. He saw a creek running through a meadow. They walked along the creek and she knelt down and said, "Look, there's a frog."

Its whole body was a way to inhale and exhale. It was all breath, like some Zen ideal. The frog lunged into the mud.

"When I was a kid," she said and told him about catching frogs with her brother. Like many of her stories, there was nothing interesting about the story she told but he was interested. The banality of the content combined with the enthusiasm of the telling was evidence that she found her life fascinating, that she was discovering this anew all the time, and this sense was infectious. She was infectious. He was infected.

They hiked up. They looked back and saw meadows spread out before mountains. They kept going and came to what looked like a pile of rocks five stories high and was actually the peak of a mountain. They followed what seemed to be a path through the scree, up to the top. When they arrived there, they found a small house. An abandoned fire lookout. An actual one. Its humility fueled his suspicion of the fire lookout they'd stayed in after they first got together, eight months before.

"It's beautiful."

It was weather-beaten. It was painted a dark, peeling green. It was lashed down to the mountain with steel cables. They went in. It had low ceilings and a small desk and a kitchen table and glass in the windows and simple graffiti etched everywhere. Initials + Initials = Love. If only it were that simple.

"I wish we could live here," she said.

"I know. But maybe we should live somewhere else together."

She bent down and looked out one of the little windows.

"I'm serious," he said. "We should move in together. Don't you want to?"

"Are you sure?"

"Sure," he said. "I'm sure."

"I just don't want you to do it because you think it's what I want. Because I know you think I want all this stuff but I don't. All I want is to be with you and for us to be like we were, like we are: unafraid."

"I'm not," he said. "I'm not afraid. That's why I'm asking. Because I want to. That's all. I want to be with you. It'll be fun. We'll get a house. A little house. It'll be great."

"I know. I know it will."

They hugged. They kissed. They stepped out of the cabin, stood on a ledge of rock that overlooked huge mountains clear-cut in elaborate patterns, and noticed a hang glider lifted by the wind. The hang glider was close enough that he could read the numbers painted white on its black wings: 45. It flew past, falling from the sky as gracefully as possible.

22

When summer came and their previous leases ended, they moved into a one-bedroom apartment across the street from a riverfront park and a Holiday Inn loading dock. The apartment was on the first floor of an old house, so there were high ceilings and crown moldings and one glass cupboard and tall windows but the place was filthy and the floors were carpet and linoleum and the kitchen really was the size of a closet and the employees of the Holiday Inn looked in their living-room windows when they took their smoke breaks. It wasn't ideal and it wasn't a whole house, like they'd hoped it would be, but the location was good and rent was very cheap.

They went to a thrift store to buy a couch. Since she still believed in *the Christian narrative*, as she called it, and preferred to do the right thing, they went to look for one at a Christian thrift store called Teen Challenge that employed troubled young people and ostensibly redeemed them via retail sales. Several living rooms worth of furniture, including four identical cushy chairs, were arranged in the parking lot. They parked and sat in all four of them, testing them out and discussing their merits.

"That's nice," she said, leaning back.

"Let's see what's inside," he said.

Inside, there were racks of clothes and shelves of mass-market paperbacks and stacks of lampshades and an end-table display of Thanksgiving knick-knacks, such as a teddy bear wearing a Pilgrim hat and gripping an unfurled American flag. They looked around and found a fifteen-dollar couch with a floral pattern.

"It's like something from Anthropologie," she said.

They agreed to get it and went to pay. There wasn't a line at the register but the cashier was turned around and occupied with a bag of receipts, so they waited and Ed noticed that there was a series of laminated photos pinned to a bulletin board beside where they stood. Along with the photos, text was printed in a whimsical font. Comic Sans or something like that. He started reading what was written beneath a photo of a girl who had highlights and looked like she'd been pregnant until recently: *My name's Miranda. I'm twenty. I was a good, happy kid. When I was fifteen, I broke my wrist playing softball. I started taking pain pills. I got hooked. By the time I was eighteen, I was mainlining heroin.* It went on but he stopped reading to tap his girlfriend and show her, since she'd think it was weird and interesting too. When he'd tapped her and was looking back to see why she hadn't responded, he saw that the cashier had turned around and that she looked like Miranda and that of course she was Miranda and that she was smiling and ready to help them.

"Hi," Miranda said. She was chipper and Ed felt sorry for her. He tried to see her gaunt and strung out in a basement apartment but he'd never done heroin and he just saw an overweight nineteen-year-old in a second-hand hoodie and a silver necklace with a dolphin pendant. "How can I help you?"

He explained.

"Do you take cards?" Taylor asked and Ed was embarrassed.

Miranda, smiling, said, yes, indeed they did. She had the temporary enthusiasm of someone who just drank a five-hour energy drink. "Sure."

Ed paid and Miranda followed him back to the furniture and helped him load the couch into the back of Taylor's SUV while Taylor looked on, and Ed wished there was a way he could tip Miranda without making things awkward. He couldn't, so he just thanked her and said, "Take care."

As he pulled out of the parking lot, he wondered which servant Miranda was. *The third one*, he thought. *She has so few talents.* Then he and Taylor went home and sat on the couch they'd bought.

"Let's be together forever," Taylor said.

"I want to. We will."

They sat there until a Holiday Inn employee came outside to smoke and made eye contact with them.

"Let's do something," she said.

They drove out of town and went for a hike up a steep canyon, alongside a deep and fast-moving creek. As they went, he stepped on a stick that popped up and hit the side of his ankle, right behind the bone, sending an explosion of pain up into his calf and down into his foot. It was the same kind of sharp pain that emanated from the tumor in his arm, except amplified. It was a new tumor, growing in his leg. Instead of telling her about it, he told her about the Kootenai Indians, who this creek was named for and who he'd recently read about online.

"They were the only tribe never to sign a treaty with the government," Ed said, "so they never got a reservation

or any land or any kind of compensation at all." He hoped
he was remembering this right. It seemed less correct the
more he said. "So they just ended up living in northwestern
Montana and northern Idaho and around there, but they just
had nothing. And so then in the '80s I think it was—or the
'70s, maybe—they just, like, took over Bonner's Ferry and set
up these checkpoints all around the town and they charged
anyone who wasn't an Indian, like, a dollar or something to
drive through. Wouldn't that make a good movie?"

"But what happened? After they set up the checkpoints
and stuff, did they get something out of it?"

"Yeah, I think so. I think they got to live on another tribe's
land. Something like that."

They came out of the canyon and the creek slowed and
calmed and at a sandy beach, they disrobed to their underwear and she counted to three. They ran and dove in and it
was so cold it erased all exterior feeling, turned all sensation
internal. It was enlivening. He was numb. They scurried out
and stood in the sun. The world was such a better place with
her around. That's all it was. That's why he was with her.

23

F or his birthday, Taylor bought tickets to a John Prine
concert being held in a university auditorium. Lots of
lost-looking elderly people were there and Ed was nervous
the entire time that he was falling for something, that John
Prine was actually a hack, that to enjoy himself would be to
be duped. He sat with Taylor in the balcony. In the row in
front of them, a pretty college girl consoled the overweight
woman who was probably her mother and who cried the
entire time. He imagined that the mother's husband had been
a huge John Prine fan, that this was one of her husband's
defining enthusiasms, and that he, her husband, was dead.
He wondered if Taylor would cry if he died and she heard a
John Prine song.

He decided to take the woman's grief as confirmation
of the music's authenticity. But why does sadness make
something true? He tried to think of a counter example and
thought of children. Children laughing and playing in the
sun. A photo of his sister as a little girl, with a little girl's
bangs and holding a toy, ignoring the camera. Maybe that's
why she was so photogenic: she could ignore that a picture
was being taken, that she would be seen in this moment
forever, a fact that contorted most people. He loved his sister
but she made him sad. This felt like a failing of his. He knew

he shouldn't pity her but how else could he place himself in relationship to her? Could he admire her? He couldn't confide in her, for example. He knew the answer—that he should just love her—but that was too simple. Sentimental, almost. Anything true is complicated. Also, as with the crying John Prine fan, sad.

Taylor put her head on his shoulder in the dark theater and the song ended and everyone clapped and the pretty girl held her mother, who sobbed silently. After the inevitable encore, Ed wanted to stop thinking, so they rode their bikes downtown to the VFW.

When he'd first moved to Missoula, the VFW had been a dive bar. As more people like him had started coming in to take advantage of the cheap drinks and the authentically blue-collar atmosphere, however, they'd added taps of local microbrews and raised their prices and hired hip young people to bartend and started charging a cover on nights when bands were playing. On this night, though, they had karaoke.

He ordered a well whiskey and later, when he was sufficiently drunk, he signed up to sing "Margaritaville," ironically, and when his friend Allison, the gutter punk who'd hosted the party where people shot air guns and who now taught at an alternative preschool, heard it was his birthday, she gave him a pin that had been affixed to her jean vest. The pin read, *Growth for the sake of growth is the ideology of the cancer cell.* The quote was attributed to Edward Abbey. He liked the quote but immediately, reflexively anticipated his father's response, should he ever see the pin affixed to his son's jacket or backpack. His father would say, *But cancer cells don't have an ideology.* Two of his dad's three brothers and both of his dad's parents had died of cancer, and he had one tumor on his arm, one in his back, one in his ankle, and who knew how many elsewhere inside him. He thanked Allison, attached the pin to the pocket of his short-sleeved collared shirt, and bought her a drink, plus one for himself.

The next morning, in the bathroom mirror, dried blood was crusted on his forehead and he vaguely remembered awaking still drunk in the middle of the night to pee and walking into the side of the open bathroom door. It had hurt but not badly and he'd gone back to bed. He rubbed the blood from off his head and revealed a perfectly vertical cut running above the small space he plucked between his eyebrows, to keep them distinct. He felt like a bad person. He had to teach in two hours. He showered and rinsed off the blood, but the cut remained. Errors can't always be undone. For those of privilege, this is always a revelation.

He wore a hat to class and hoped no one would notice, but while giving them yet another lecture about how they really had to do the assigned reading, about how if you don't want to read and write there's really no point in being in college, because that's the whole point of college and there are plenty of equally worthy and much cheaper places to spend one's youth, such as working a job or learning a trade, Ed removed the hat and saw everyone see the cut running up the center of his head.

"Oh my God," said a pretty girl who sat in the back and was probably the biggest slut in her dorm, "are you, like, becoming Harry Potter?"

Everyone laughed.

He remembered the last time someone had made the association, at Nimrod, the summer before. "Who's that?"

He was trying to make a joke, to find a way out of his embarrassment, but this time, no one laughed.

The cut on his forehead faded but never did disappear. His cut was a scar.

24

Ed went home to see his family. He was in Montana, Colorado, Georgia, and South Carolina within a fourteen-hour period. He went to bed in the room he'd grown up in. As a boy, he'd shared the room with his brother, who slept now in their father's study, on a pull-out couch. The tumors made it difficult to sleep. They sent pain surging inside him. Since Ed couldn't sleep, he crawled out the window, onto the roof of the back porch, and lit a cigarette, as he had done so many times while in high school. While he smoked, his father went out in the backyard. What was his father doing? He expected now to witness his father light a joint or at least a cigarette or sit on the back steps and weep, but his father just took out the trash and went back inside. Ed wasn't sure if he was disappointed or relieved. He decided to have a second cigarette.

In the morning, his mom asked him to go with her on a walk. They walked through the lush Southern streets. He'd forgotten how hot and humid it was there, how tropical. Untended yards were overwhelmed with vegetation. He'd been a boy here but he barely remembered any of it. It was like something that had happened to someone else and that he'd been told about and that he had largely forgotten. He'd ridden his bike and had friends and had built a tree house and had smoked cigarettes at the park and had played soccer but he couldn't inhabit how any of that had felt. It wasn't like yesterday or last year, which was hazy but which he could feel. Childhood wasn't even a memory. It was a concept.

Before they'd gone even a block, his mom said, "I have to tell you something." Then she told him that she'd been married before she married his father. "I was in college," she said. "My mom had just died. I was only twenty."

"Who was he?"

"His dad was this rich man from Milwaukee and Don—his name was Don. Don was just this really interesting guy. Kind of wild. It was the '60s. We lived on a horse farm."

"A horse farm?"

"It was an hour outside of Burlington. But then he got in this car wreck and went into a coma and when he came out, he was never the same. He was just really mean and I was so young and I didn't know what to do, so I left him. I went to Boston. Where I met your dad."

"You did?" He was her child. She'd given birth to him and when he was being born, when he was coming out of her, he'd broken his collarbone. She was as abstract as an emotion to him: he could feel her but did not understand anything about her. "Why are you telling me this?"

"Your brother, he was in New York for some conference thing and he had dinner with my cousin Nathan and I guess Nathan brought him up, assuming you guys already knew. He just said something like, 'So what ever happened to your mom's first husband?'" She laughed slightly, bemused. "So then your brother knew and I thought you should too." She'd been beautiful, Ed could see. "I love you," she said.

"That's so weird. What happened to Don?"

"Oh, I don't really know. I mean, we lost touch. He was working for his dad, last I heard, in Milwaukee."

He imagined Don: an angry man, a lonely man, an overweight man, a man who tucked his T-shirts into his shorts and thought he looked distinguished, a ruined man, a man abandoned by his wife, in his time of need.

Later on in his visit, while he was helping his mom clear out a closet full of things he'd accumulated in high school—back issues of *Punk Planet* magazine, old soccer jerseys, ugly dress clothes—his mother asked him if he wanted a ring.

"One of your grandmother's rings," she said. "To propose, in case you want to." She went to the shelf at the top of her closet and took down a small box. Ed didn't trust her. She could make him do anything. "She got it in Brazil. When your father was growing up there, I think. It has emeralds." She opened the box and showed him what was inside. It looked fragile. "Diamonds and emeralds."

"It's nice."

"Take it." She gave it to him. "So you can, if you want to."

He took the velvet box that contained the ring to his childhood bedroom and zipped it into the smallest and outermost pocket of his backpack. Then he went out to the back porch and watched his sister play basketball in the driveway, with some little girls who'd recently moved in next door. The girls were maybe five and eight. The girls tried to explain to Ellie how to play H.O.R.S.E. She didn't understand and they laughed at her and Ed felt overwhelmed by how hard her life must be, being laughed at by children, too ignorant even to understand why.

He watched her. One of the girls missed a shot from the baseline and the ball hit the trunk of his mother's Volvo, which was parked in the garage. The ball hit the trunk with a thud and bounced down the driveway, which was steep. His sister ran after the ball, toward the street, and Ed imagined a car coming around the corner too fast, hitting his sister, undermining the lives of everyone involved, but Ellie returned proudly, with the ball in her hands, ten seconds later. How had his parents—their parents—dealt with her condition? How had it shaped them? What were their lives like? Who were these people? His heart felt weak, unsure. The future was something he couldn't prevent.

25

After Ed graduated from the graduate creative writing program, the only job he could get, after two months of trying, was as a prep cook and baker in a warehouse in a strip mall in a town called Lolo. Lewis and Clark had passed through the area before the town existed and now it was a jumble of gas stations and streets without sidewalks and houses with fake wells in the front yard and fast food restaurants and an out-of-business Chinese restaurant called Wok E. Mountain.

In the warehouse, he sliced meat and cheese and baked bread and scones and cookies. The only other people in the warehouse with him all day were a single middle-aged Christian woman who'd dyed her hair an uneven shade of red and who silently packed coffee in plastic baggies from eight in the morning until four in the afternoon and a married guy who wore cargo pants and listened to an Internet radio station that aggregated songs by an algorithm that rewarded mediocrity and who roasted coffee at a huge, loud, Italian machine. It was like a circle of hell you'd find in an allegory. He didn't know what the allegory would be about but the word *capitalism* kept coming to mind. His dad was an economist, after all.

The food that he made during the day waited in containers overnight and then, after he'd arrived back at work the next morning, was shipped, via minivan, to a coffee bar twelve miles away. The coffee bar was two blocks from where he lived with Taylor and it seemed ridiculous that he came to this strip mall from his house and that the things he spent all day making then went back the other way, from where he'd come. His father, being an economist, had taught his son to value efficiency above all else. But there he was.

He didn't need to be there, but he worked there, in the loud warehouse. He spent twenty minutes plucking the stems off of sweet, hot peppers. He ladled vinegar-soaked vegetables into a French blender with a name—Robot Coupe—that he'd pronounced like it was written in English and then he'd imagined robots in a sports car and then his supervisor, a sad middle-aged Bowdoin College graduate, had corrected him, softening the consonants, and he tried to tell himself that everything was all right but he wasn't convincing. The world felt like a system for humiliating him. He cut six heads of lettuce and then spilled it all on the dirty cement floor. He went through a drive-thru and bought three tacos from a place called Taco Time and ate them in his hot car, parked in the strip-mall parking lot, during his lunch break. Then he rolled fifty-six loaves of sourdough bread by hand and sliced some ham, some roast beef, and lots of turkey.

When he was in high school and guilty about his privilege, he'd fantasized about one day inheriting his parents' money and giving a substantial portion of it to his family's by then elderly housekeeper. She was as short as a child and had bright white dentures and he always hugged her when he saw her now. When they embraced, he'd smell her hair and it smelled like a thrift store. When he got off work today, Ed decided, he'd send her some of his savings. Not a lot. Maybe a hundred bucks. A nice gesture. An amount that could be appreciated but wasn't condescending. He'd put it in a card. He'd write "Happy Belated Birthday!" inside.

When he got off and was driving past mountains and rivers and strip malls on his way home, he realized how embarrassing his plan was and instead just went home to the apartment he shared with Taylor and noticed that some-one had pinned a photocopy of the Constitution to the wall between his and his neighbor's back door. All he read was *We the people* before he went in.

From inside, he saw Taylor through the huge living-room windows, on the front porch, typing on her laptop. She looked like a wife and that meant she looked like his wife. He still had the ring his mother had given him in a box, at the bottom of his sock drawer. He went through the kitchen and into the living room and stuck his head out the window and said, "Boo," halfheartedly.

"Oh, hey," she said. "How was your day?"

"Good," he said. "I missed you the whole time."

She didn't respond. She was engrossed in her computer.

"What are you doing?" he said.

"Writing."

He pulled his head back in the window.

26

They showered together until the hot water ran out, then wrapped themselves in towels and went to the bedroom. On the way, they passed by a pair of tall, open windows. As they did, Ed made eye contact with a male employee of the Holiday Inn across the street. The employee was on break, smoking at a picnic table, and the employee waved. It was creepy. Ed did not respond. He followed his girlfriend and found her in her towel, on the bed.

"Don't you want me?"

He came to her, lay beside her. The blinds were drawn. The world was somewhere else, with the Holiday Inn employee. The bedroom was dark and cool and her body was warm and soft and close and they made love. When she came back from the bathroom, Taylor sat on the bed and told Ed she believed she was pregnant.

"Not from just now," she said. "My period was supposed to start five days ago."

"OK," Ed said. "It's OK." She leaned into him. He held her and he told her he loved her but he didn't believe her. She had a history of false pregnancies. "I mean, you've been in this position before, haven't you? And everything worked out fine."

"I know, I know. But this is different and I can't..." She couldn't say what he knew she couldn't say: that she couldn't have an abortion. "But I would," she said. "If you wanted."

"I know, but I don't want you to. We'll deal with whatever happens. It's what everyone does. We're as good as them. As everyone."

She apologized and he assured her and he told her he'd take her to CVS and buy her a test.

"I'm going to take care of you."

Ed knew it was true but had no idea what it meant. Ed thought of the Holiday Inn employee, who knew what his girlfriend looked like in a towel but nothing else about her. He tried to think of himself as a father but could only imagine his own dad. He tried to think of the future but came up with a pastiche of the past. He tried to remember the past but came up with nothing, so he thought about a house he'd recently seen while riding his bike. It was a regular house. A white bungalow with light brown or dark gray or navy blue trim. He had a bad memory. The grass was green and the house was tidy. Old but undamaged and unrusted patio furniture was arranged on the back deck as carefully as the objects in an art installation.

The house was in one corner of a huge lot. Several rows of metal storage units occupied the rest of the space. The storage units were as immaculate as the house. The storage units were all painted beige and they all had doors that were made of strips of metal. The doors were the kind that roll up when you pull up on the handle near the poured-concrete ground.

Chain-link fencing topped with barbed wire surrounded the house and the storage units—the entire lot. The barbed wire ran in three parallel strands set at an angle meant to either keep people out or in, depending on the direction it leaned.

The way he remembered it, the barbed wire around this house leaned in, toward the house, as if to keep people from escaping. But that made no sense: the barbed wire must've been installed to protect the stuff in the storage units, to ensure safety for everyone's leftover stuff. And then the owners must've decided they might as well protect themselves too, while they were at it.

He could see how it happened, he guessed, but he had a hard time explaining it to himself. A house kept inside barbed wire seemed like a symbol for something. It indicated that you can trap yourself by being protective.

"What are you thinking about?" she said.

"Nothing," he said. "Just about where we will live."

"What about it?"

"That it will be expensive," Ed said.

The idea of punishing her appealed to him, so long as he could deny that he was doing it. He wanted her to distrust herself, not him. It was a way to maintain control.

"You're just worried that it won't be easy," Taylor said.

They dressed and went to CVS, which was in an otherwise unoccupied strip mall with a parking lot the size of a square city block. It should've been ugly but there were mountains behind the building and the mountains made everything impressive. They were why Ed lived there.

Ed parked. It was a bright, dry, and hot day. When they walked to the automatic door, they held hands. The store had the linoleum flooring and drop ceiling of a public school. The space was too big for the store. The aisles were too wide. The pregnancy tests were beside the condoms, which mocked him. Why hadn't they used one? Because they made sex feel less like sex and more like a dangerous chore. That they were here now was strong evidence of the unreliability of feelings, which only tell us about ourselves. The world is much bigger than that. And it was getting bigger, with more children every minute. They did not buy the store brand of test, though they discussed doing so.

When they got home, Taylor went into the bathroom and closed the door. While she was in there, Ed checked his email. His closest friend, who he'd lived with in college and then in Chicago a few years after they graduated, had written him an email with the subject "Chillfest." In it, Ed's friend said that he and his girlfriend had bought tickets to come visit him in Montana. Ed had talked to his friend about the visit but had forgotten about it. Ed needed to pay stronger attention.

"Hey," Taylor said from behind him.

He turned to her. She looked at him the way she had when they first met and would see each other across a bar.

"It was green," she said. She did not look like a mother. She was too calm, too young. "Which I guess means I'm pregnant."

He managed to hold her, when she came to him and cried, joyfully, but while he did, he couldn't help but think of himself. He couldn't help but think of the tumor inside him and the human inside her and about how the two were related. He tried to think of this thought as being beautiful. He thought of his sister. She was beautiful. Though her life was small and hard, he thought, it contained a kind of beauty.

He managed to say, "I'm so happy," and when Taylor stopped crying, she whispered something into his ear. Ed couldn't hear what it was.

Ed couldn't hear her and this meant he had tumors in his brain and this meant he would likely lose his memory and maybe more of his brain function and maybe he'd even develop dementia or some other mental illness and his child would inherit his condition and his brain tumors and his hearing and memory loss and, as a result, his child's life would be hard and it would be his fault. Taylor, Ed thought, was beautiful but her child would be flawed and difficult and deaf and it would be because of him. He would do it. He thought, *I already have.*

27

E d opened his laptop and scrolled through a document, ransackednew24.doc, the latest draft of the novel he was working on and which he was calling *Ransacked*. He'd been working on it for four years. It began, "Life is a last chance. I had mine. Now I'm here. Now I'm being held in the McLean County Jail and Clarence, my cellmate, seems like he's lived here forever."

It was a novel about homelessness, as narrated by an accused and jailed pedophile. It was false and tame and Ed hated it. He'd revised and rewritten it endlessly, but only ever made it more convoluted and clever, attributes that he couldn't admit were flaws, even though he knew they were.

He couldn't bear to read it and admit that he needed to abandon it, so he packed the fake cigarette and hoped being high would allow him to see it from a new, skewed angle and imagine a way out of what felt like a three-hundred-page error. He deleted a paragraph, fixed the shape of a few sentences, and closed his laptop. He'd gotten lost inside his brain and he had to escape, so he resolved to stop working on his novel. To abandon it forever. He was done, he decided. There was nothing more he could do, no reason to continue.

What Ed wanted to do was write a love story. He wanted to but he couldn't, because he knew Taylor would read it. It was going to be a story and he wanted it to be good, so it would have to be sad. The love would have to go wrong somewhere near the end. And he loved her. He didn't want her to start thinking that something had gone wrong. Or was about to. So he didn't write it. Wouldn't.

But it was an early fall afternoon and Taylor was in her fiction workshop—she had almost a year left in the creative writing program—and now he didn't know how to occupy his day, so he just sat on the thrift-store couch in the living room and rolled a tiny, personal joint—he wasn't going to get that stoned, he wasn't going to waste a bunch of weed—and opened the window and let the outside inside and got slightly high.

When he thought of Taylor, he thought of his love for her. He suspected he'd ruin it soon. Maybe he already had. It didn't take much. You start corrupting something like that, and there's no going back. It's like watching dye disperse, slowly, in water. He didn't want to see that. He went out on the porch to read.

Ed was reading a nonfiction book about a county in northeastern Montana that had consistently elected communists to local posts in the '20s but he was having a hard time connecting the sentences together. He forgot the one he'd just read by the time he'd made it halfway through the next one. It wasn't much of a problem to have, not compared to those of Montana's long-lost communists.

He kept trying. He read that in Sheridan County, in 1931, thirty-one children attended the local Young Communist Training School and that the next year a fourteen-year-old girl died of appendicitis and that she was given a Bolshevik funeral by her fellow Young Pioneers and that the funeral took place on a farm and that the audience sang "The Internationale" (*Stand up, damned of the Earth / Stand up, prisoners of starvation*) and that a red scarf was dropped into the open grave, onto the lowered casket, but that was as much as he could decipher. But that seemed like a lot. Like too much.

Were a hammer and sickle engraved on her gravestone, beneath her dates: *Janis Salisbury: 1918–1932*? He wanted to know.

28

He walked to the river that was across the street from where they lived. There was a low retaining wall painted with a bad mural whose theme seemed to be River Wildlife. There was a snake and a frog and some other stuff. A local artist-in-the-schools had painted it with some seventh graders last summer. These were the kinds of thing he knew about the world. It was disheartening.

Lots of people were out on the river path and in the grass beside it and on both sides of the river and even floating down the river in inner tubes. Ed walked for a while, then went and sat in the grass between the path, a parking lot, downtown's main bridge, and the far side of the hotel he lived across from. A family was having a blast near some picnic tables. He watched them for clues.

There was a mother, a father, a son, and a daughter. The kids were maybe five and eight, respectively. Ed wasn't great at knowing which characteristics corresponded to which ages of a child. When do they learn to talk, for example?

His girlfriend was pregnant but their child would never be as beautiful as her. He would be the father.

The father of the family was the kind of guy who sells mattresses for a living. He didn't seem very well rested. He kicked a big purple ball around with his kids. The kind of ball you pull from a slot near the bottom of one of those big cages full of brightly colored balls at the grocery store. The kids were trying to kick the ball as far as they could. They were trying to impress their dad. "Watch this," they kept saying, and then they would just kick the ball. They were having fun. The father was kicking it too.

Ed felt weird about watching them, so he tried to read—he'd brought a book, a novel about an alcoholic—but couldn't, so instead he pretended. It was difficult to pretend, because now he was just looking at a sheet of paper, which was boring, so he was relieved when he heard an exclamation from one of the kids and looked over and saw that they were all looking up at the sky. Ed looked up at the sky too and saw the purple ball caught high up in the branches of a really tall pine tree. It looked like a tumor in a network of nerves. Or that's the comparison he made because he had tumors growing in the network of his nerves. His tumors were smooth and egg-shaped and benign and they were growing inside him. They wouldn't kill him. They would replace his brain, slowly, he believed, but did not really know.

He didn't want to know, so he hadn't had a brain scan. He didn't want to have one, so he didn't tell his girlfriend that everything sounded muffled, that he kept hearing phantom voices that sounded like voices on a TV with the volume on as low as it goes. He didn't turn his music up. He didn't ask her to repeat things. He tried to read her lips but couldn't see how movement can make sound.

"Daddy, it's stuck up there," yelled the father's son to his father. The father's daughter was talking about it too and the father promised he'd knock it down. The son handed the father a soccer ball they hadn't been using. The father

punted it up and, after a few tries, the purple ball came down
and the soccer ball disappeared. It disappeared into the tree.
Ed couldn't see it now. It was stuck by the trunk, the father
explained to the kids, and it would be hard to get down. Then
the mother, who'd been watching the river with her back to
her family, came over. The mother looked really athletic.
Whatever her husband saw in her—whatever attracted him
to her—was invisible to Ed. When the kids explained the
situation to her, she looked pleased.

Ed tried to go back and figure out the book he couldn't
read but he was distracted by the family and how they would
solve their problem. They were looking at the soccer ball
they'd punted into a tree in a successful effort to dislodge
a purple novelty ball that they'd been kicking around. They
did this—looked at the ball in the tree—for a long time, until
the father/husband announced that it was time to go home,
it was getting late.

"It's bedtime soon," the mother said.

The son protested: "How can it be night if it's still
light out?"

No one answered him. The parents started to walk off.
The daughter followed. The son didn't. He kept looking, until
the soccer ball fell from the tree, hit the ground, bounced
high. "Look," the son called out triumphant, then gathered
the ball and ran after his family to show them.

Ed sat there for a long time, not reading, thinking of
the family and of all the people who were barely alive, who
live in houses and think about work or television and have
families and drink Coors Light while they watch *SNL* alone
in a living room on a Saturday night, as his dad did. It felt
like a sad thought and his sadness seemed condescending.

He reminded himself of the limitations of his imagination: he didn't know what it was to be his dad.

His dad had grown up in Missouri and Indiana and then moved, via steamship, to the northeast of Brazil, where his father's father—Ed's grandfather—worked with local farmers, taught them modern agricultural techniques. As a result, Ed's dad spoke Portuguese. Later, he'd learned Spanish in Colombia and French in Switzerland and German from listening to a short-wave radio in his study, while his children slept. His father had seen the Kinks play in a Washington DC high-school auditorium. His dad was married to his mom. His dad had three kids. Ed was one of them. Ed's dad had another son and he had a daughter, who was the oldest child and who was retarded.

Ed spent a lot of time trying to figure out what his dad thought of this last fact. If he could figure out what his dad thought of it, he could figure out what his dad felt about it. He didn't have much to go on but his mother had told him a story: when Ed's sister was two, his mother and father had begun to suspect that something was wrong with her because she had trouble learning new words. She knew twenty of them but the learning of a new one necessitated the forgetting of an old one. Ed wished he had a list of the words. His parents took her to the doctor and found out that, yes, it was in fact likely that she had an intellectual disability. After that, his father refused to go to any of the many appointments that were set up to diagnose her condition more specifically. "He didn't want to know," his mother told him when he was home five or so Christmases ago and they were walking the dog and she was telling him this story for the first time. Ed imagined that his dad didn't want to know because he felt that her retardation was his fault. He'd made her and he'd made her that way.

Ed could see how that would be, but Ed didn't know much about his dad and Ed wondered if maybe his dad thought of the little information he divulged about himself as a disguise that he couldn't change out of. He looked familiar—like a dad—but no one knew who he was. No one recognized him.

As Ed thought about all of this, the sun went down reluctantly.

29

As part of a series for second-year MFA students, Taylor gave a reading at a bar that had recently been renovated, converting it from a dive into the kind of place where late-middle-age women meet up for appetizers and white wine, where people in their thirties are careful to not quite get drunk. It was a Sunday evening. With a few exceptions—two people on a first date, a man flipping through the news-paper—everyone there was affiliated with the program. They sat at tables, drank drinks, and looked at the stage, where a 26-year-old fiction student who wrote florid stories about grotesque Southerners introduced Taylor.

"She looks like she couldn't be sweeter," he said in his affected Alabama accent, reading off multiple sheets of paper. "I mean, look at her."

The audience laughed, and Taylor, who held Ed's hand under the table, looked deeply pained and embarrassed.

"But in workshop," the student continued, now more than five minutes into his introduction, "she looms like a threat. She sits there quietly, patiently, saying nothing while we all go around and around, critiquing whatever we're reading, trying to figure out what's right and what's wrong—and all the while just waiting for Taylor, after we've all talked our-selves out, to speak up. Her comments always come at the end, and they always explain what matters about the story we're reading. Not the 'how' of the story—the mechanics, the plot, the language, whatever—but the 'why.' The point—and whether or not it was worth making.

"And that's the thing about Taylor's fiction: it was always worth making. As I'm sure you will now see."

The audience clapped, and Taylor walked with her head down to the stage, where she awkwardly hugged her introducer, adjusted the microphone stand, and thanked everyone for coming.

"I'm going to read something new," she said. "It's called 'The Executive.' It's part of a novel I'm working on. I think."

Taylor took a sip of her soda water, then started:

"Casey pushed a shopping cart across the huge parking lot. Her daughter looked back at her, bawling, kicking her legs, squirming in the top part of the cart, where Casey had kept fruit and other fragile items before she had a kid. It was extremely hot. 102°, according to a bank she'd passed on her way to the store. But what does a bank know about the weather?

"*It's OK, baby. It's OK.*

"Besides her daughter, the cart contained groceries and diapers and a container of three tennis balls and two new tennis rackets, because she didn't know how to play and her friend Jenny had promised to teach her, if she got the equipment. It sounded good, like something to do. Something carefree and pointless. They were meeting at 3:00.

"Casey drove through the little Montana city—over the river, along the mountains, past a park and a school and a courthouse and a bakery. It was as straightforward and contained as the setting of a children's book. Casey was on her way to her parents' house, where she'd grown up and where she was staying. Where she shared a room with her daughter.

"Casey's parents lived on the city's rural fringe, in a gated community. As Casey pulled into the cul-de-sac, she saw a new vehicle in front of their neighbors' house. A huge, lifted truck. On the tailgate, in airbrush, someone had written 'The Executive.' It was funny to her.

"*Look, it's the Executive*, she said to her daughter, who didn't talk yet, in her baby voice. *Say hi to the Executive.*

"Inside, her parents were watching TV. A football game. It was Saturday, Casey realized. Her dad nodded hello. Her mom got up, came close, shook the baby's foot, and said, *You wanna come to gramma?*

"Casey gave her daughter to her mother and went out to get what she'd bought."

Taylor looked up. "OK," she said. "Here's a break." She looked like she was counting to three, inside her head. Then she started again:

"The tennis courts were right on the river. Casey stood on the side closest to it, with a view of the park and of Jenny, who was touching her toes.

"*It's so weird you're back*, Jenny said.

"*I guess*, Casey said.

"*So what happened?*

"*With what?*

"*What's his name? Your husband?*

"*Sam?*

"*Yeah.* Jenny laughed, sat down on the court, changed stretches. *Sam.*

"*He was just, I don't know...* Casey stood there, not stretching. *I don't know if I want to do this. Play tennis.*

"*What? Are you serious?*

"*I don't even know how.*

"*That's the point. I'm going to teach you.*

"For the next half hour, they sort of hit the ball back and forth. It seemed like it should be easy but was actually hard, which made it frustrating. Plus, it was so fucking hot. Afterward, they walked down to the river, took off their shoes and socks, and waded in.

"When Casey dove into the cold and clean water, she'd never felt such a sudden change. When she came up, she was frighteningly far down the river and the river was pulling her further. She swam as hard as she could but moved no closer to shore. Casey tried harder but only felt herself being brought under. She surfaced and tried to scream and water filled her mouth. She went under for a second and rested and panicked and popped back out. Casey felt she was nowhere in the tumult of the river, of the water that moved without a bottom. She was too tired to swim but she did, downriver, at a slight angle. And then the water seemed to slow and Casey somehow felt sand underneath her, scraping her shins. She scrambled until she found herself in waist-high water, near the bank, near the minor league baseball field. She stumbled to shore and lay back, heaving. As she calmed, she began to shiver.

"When she sat up, Casey noticed a bright blue tent nearby in the tall grass. She heard a family riding bicycles down the river trail. She heard a woman talking on her cell phone to her child: *I told you to call me when you got home.*

"Here Casey was, back on earth. All she had to do was borrow the woman's cell phone and call Jenny, who screamed when she found out Casey was fine and said she'd just got

off the phone with 911 but she'd call them back and cancel
and come get her.

"*Just meet me by the indoor swim place*, Casey said.

"While she waited in her soaked T-shirt and shorts, she
watched parents bringing their children in and out of the
municipal aquatics center. She watched them for clues about
her future. She should bring Lucy here, she knew. She would
and then Lucy would join a swimming team and then, for
the next decade, she would drive Lucy around from to swimming meets and practices and tournaments and Lucy would
become a good swimmer, a fit kid. That would be Casey's
life and that was why she'd left her husband. That was why
she'd told him, *This is crazy, and I'm not going to do it*. That's
what she meant, though she'd had a hard time explaining it:
that she didn't want to be that kind of person, so safe with
their life. So concerned about what's coming, so resigned to
disaster, so willing to turn everything into a burden, even their
daughter. Even her—his wife. He dreaded what was coming.
He worried about insurance and money. How will we pay
when things start to go wrong? That's the kind of thing he
wanted to think about, and Casey couldn't understand why.

"He'd quit his job as a reporter for the local alt weekly
and taken a position writing marketing materials for a local
branch of the state university. He said he did it for the bene-
fits, but Casey knew he did it so he could punish her, so he
could blame his misery on her. Her: she'd had the child. Now
the child never slept and always cried. That's how it seemed,
anyway, in their little house in Denver, where she tried to
survive until her husband came home from work and started
to complain, thinly cloaking accusations as apologies.

"*I'm sorry. I just didn't know it would be like this.*

"Like what?

"Never mind. I'm sorry.

"Casey's husband, Sam, had grown up in Chicago and attended an expensive private school, located downtown. Around the time they were breaking up, he'd told her about how they'd played their official high-school baseball games— wearing uniforms, with coaches—in a crummy city park and how they got heckled by neighborhood kids, who hated them for their wealth and for how bad they were. When he told her this story, Casey thought—or hoped—that he was trying to say to her, *I'm sorry for being so deliberate, so afraid.* It was as close as he ever got to expressing actual, honest remorse. It was very far away.

"When Jenny pulled up, she was smoking a menthol cigarette.

"Holy shit, Jenny said. *I'm so happy to see you. I thought you were a goner!*

"Me, too. Can I bum one of those?

"Hell yeah. And you probably need a drink."

Taylor stopped again, explained there was now another break, and continued:

"Casey drank a bottle of beer in Jenny's shower, the hot water turned all the way up and the cold water not even on, pretending it was a tropical waterfall. When she got out, she borrowed a denim dress and dried her hair. Then they walked to the bar. It was ten at night, and the sun was just going down. Her mom texted to say Casey's daughter had gone to bed and to ask when Casey would be home. Casey only responded *Thanks.*

"According to a flyer taped to the door guy's table, four bands were playing for a two-dollar cover. While she paid,

Casey could hear one of the bands in the room in the back, getting ready. Someone played the drums by himself, testing out how they sounded. Casey and Jenny got drinks and went to go watch.

"The singer wore a hunting cap and a camouflage jacket and bright red lipstick and had a mustache. The guitar player wore a polo shirt with a popped collar and round glasses. The bass player, a guy, wore a woman's white wig. The drummer wore Ray-Bans. The keyboard player, who looked Philippine, was a cute girl wearing a baseball cap.

"Everyone else in the audience looked about as dressed up, as though they'd all picked a part to play and had found outfits for it and would now perform. In her denim dress, Casey had the sinking feeling that she was the same. She wanted to leave but she hadn't even finished her drink and maybe the band would be good, despite everything.

"While they waited, Casey and Jenny talked. They'd grown up here together, gone to high school and college here together, before Casey moved to Seattle for college and then to Denver because she wanted to, before she fell in love and got married and had a daughter and left her husband.

"*Who are all these people?* Jenny said.

"*I thought maybe you knew, since you've been around.*

"*It feels really, I don't know, aristocratic or something. Set apart.*

"*Privileged*, Casey said.

"The band started to play their first song. It was an unfaithful cover of a Beyoncé song. The band took it and twisted it, to demonstrate their lack of pretension while also being sure to show that they knew better than to merely imitate the popular, the common denominator. Midway through, the cute keyboard player rapped badly, clumsily, about 'boys.'

"When it was over, they left and went to a bar where the bartender knew Jenny by name.

"*Vodka tonic?* he said.

"Jenny gave him a thumbs up.

"*And for you?*

"*The same.* When the bartender was gone, Casey said, *Holy shit, this is so much better.*

"A few older men lingered at the far end of the bar. A few older women sat at the gambling machines. A small group of punks played pool in the back. The lights could've been lower, but the digital jukebox was playing one of her favorites, a Martina McBride song she could still remember first hearing in fifth grade, at Bible camp.

"They drank and got drunk and when they went outside for a cigarette, there was a lifted white truck. Casey went around to look at the back, to see if she was right.

"*No way*, she said, finally having fun, finally loose in her life, relieved to see how unlikely things can be. *The Executive's here.*

"Casey explained the coincidence to Jenny, and they decided they'd find him, as a kind of joke. Before they could, he came outside.

"*Hey*, he said. *You like my truck?*

"They'd been pointing at it and talking about it. They turned to him. He was short but strong. He wore a baseball cap. Though his face was somewhat obscured by the brim, which was curved perfectly, Casey could tell he was hand-some. He removed a cigarette from his pack and lit it.

"*I was just telling her*, Casey said, *that I saw your truck earlier.*

"*So do you like it? Or is it too much?* he laughed, sort of shyly. *You can be honest.*

"*No, no, I like it.*

"*It's just a hobby*, he said. *You get into working on cars and the next thing you know...* He pointed at the truck, which had the presence of some other kind of thing, like a boat or a building.

"Casey and Jenny stepped on their cigarettes.

"*Maybe I'll see you inside*, he said. He was speaking to Casey, and later he came and found her, sat right beside her and started talking to her about how pretty she was.

"*I'm drunk*, she said.

"*You're fine*, he said. *You're having fun.*

"*Not that much. Maybe you can give me a ride.*

"Jenny tried to stop her, but what did Jenny know?

"*I know what you're saying*, Casey said, *but it's what I want.*

"He lowered a little set of stairs for her and helped her up into the truck.

"*So where are we going?* he said.

"*Wherever you want.*

"He took her to the house across from her parents, not that she told him that. He lived with three other guys, at least one of whom seemed to a be a drug dealer based on who he was talking to (two tattooed Asian men, a guy in a tie-dyed hoodie) in the kitchen when Casey and The Executive came in the house around 2:00. The Executive led her by the hand up to his room. It was almost empty, and the bed was neatly made. She saw that this was a mistake and also that it was too late. She tried not to think of it as rape, but he fucked her even though she didn't want him to, even though she did whisper *Stop*, though not very loud and only once, afraid of how he might react if he heard her.

"After he came on her ass, he fell asleep and Casey walked across the cul-de-sac, snuck into her parents' house, checked on her child, got in bed, and fell asleep. In her dream, none of this had happened."

Taylor folded the paper and spoke into the mic. "That's all I have for now," she said. "Thanks."

When everyone stopped applauding, people went to get drinks but Ed waited for her, at their table. When she got there, he told her how much he admired it.

"It was amazing," he said. "I didn't know you were working on a novel. I'm so proud of you."

She looked at him with confusion, almost like they'd never met, and said, "Thanks."

When Taylor went to speak to one of her professors, Ed went to the bar and ordered a whiskey. Over the next three hours, while she tried to hide the fact that she wasn't drinking and was pregnant, he ended up getting drunker than he should've and she was annoyed with him for leaving her alone in her sobriety and they got in an argument and while they were walking home, he told her—he couldn't remember the exact words—something about how he wanted to have his own life, even though they lived together and she was pregnant and everything. Not that he didn't want to be a part of everything, not that he wasn't going to stay with her forever, he assured her. Then he tried to make her understand but she refused to listen and went to sleep in her clothes on the couch, sobbing but trying to suppress it.

3O

B efore sunrise, while he waited until it was time to leave
    for work, Ed watched a documentary about heroin
addicts. He watched the movie on mute because he was
afraid he was going deaf and worried that in order to hear
it, he'd have to turn the volume up to a level that would
wake up Taylor, who was still asleep in the other room.
Cameras filmed people sneaking into buildings, shooting up in laundry rooms, negotiating with johns, eating
at Sbarro, walking down the street, loitering in stairwells,
visiting their forlorn parents. The documentary kept stalling
because he was watching it online and they stole Internet
from the Holiday Inn across the street, which meant their
connection was tenuous.

He was twenty-nine and he liked to watch people shoot
drugs into their arms on YouTube while he ate the Safeway
version of Cheerios. He believed this had something to do
with being afraid of, but interested in, death. He'd never done
heroin. He was a coward.

Despite his efforts, the bedroom door opened and Taylor
came out wearing only striped underwear and a green tank top.

"I was having a dream," she told him.

She looked like she was still having it. She was blond
and small, and her eyes were almost closed. She elicited

compassion. She was pregnant, but it didn't show. It had only been a week or two.

"It was from when I was, like, seven or something. It was a dream but it was true. It was when we lived in the desert and my dad told me that someone had built this huge water-park place a couple hours away. Near Vegas or something." Her eyes saw only what was inside her brain. "And so my family, we drove across all this sand and it was so hot and then we got there and saw that the whole thing had been abandoned before it was even finished." She'd told him this story before. She was always telling him stories like this, stories that had no point but were loaded with indecipherable meaning. "There were all of these huge poured-concrete pools that were empty. Dry. And there were sections of bright, sun-bleached waterslide pipe snaking across the sand." It sounded like she was mumbling but he knew she wasn't. "And I was just standing at a chain-link fence in the middle of the desert in my bikini while these big guard dogs barked at me."

"Go back to sleep," he said, getting up from his computer, taking her hand. It was warm and relaxed and blood pumped through it. "Come here." She was unconscious enough to be obedient. He led her back to the bedroom, to the bed.

She sat on the edge and said, "I love you."

"I love you, too."

She got back under the covers and curled up and turned away from him. "It was weird," she said. She flipped her long hair away from her neck and above her head, as though she expected him to curl up behind her and hold her. He wasn't going to. He loved her compulsively, and so his feelings for her felt coerced and he guarded his affection, rationed it. "It was scary," she said.

He was scared. He'd finally scheduled an appointment to have his brain scanned to determine whether or not tumors had begun to grow inside his head, on his cranial nerves, and the appointment was scheduled for two that afternoon. For months now a hiss of static in his ears made other people's speech sound mumbled and he was always turning the music up too loud at work and he couldn't make out most of the dialogue in the new Roman Polanski movie he and his girlfriend had seen in the theater. He had been trying to read lips to compensate for all this. He got up from the bed.

She was still turned away from him but she could feel him leaving. "Where are you going?"

"I have work," he said. "Go back to sleep." He wanted to get back in bed with her but knew he couldn't. "Dream about me."

Then he went out into the cold morning and sat in his car while it warmed up. He packed his one-hitter and took two hits and everything seemed more meaningful when he drove through the tidy downtown, past mountains and rivers, and arrived at the Lolo strip mall where he worked. He went in and put a pot of water on a hot plate while he removed his jacket, sweatpants, gloves, and hat. Then he stuffed his clothes into his locker. Having a locker made him feel like he'd never fully finished high school and also like he was an actual blue-collar worker. He baked and cooked for a coffee bar named an untranslatable French phrase. He'd spent a lot of time using his mostly forgotten high school French trying to decode it, before deciding that "the Minor Outsider" was the best he could do.

He changed from his tennis shoes into a pair of clogs that he'd bought at the mall. When the water boiled, he made a cup of coffee with it. Then he carried his mug through the bakery and said good morning to the coffee roaster, who was writing in a notebook, and he said good morning to the middle-aged Christian lady who packed the beans. It was quiet in the warehouse, and his concerns were far away, and so this, he decided, would be his favorite part of the day. He did his best to remain in this quiet moment, with coffee and silence and extremely high ceilings and an open loading-dock door that revealed green trees and the back of an apartment building and a sky that was starting to blush blue with the sunrise.

31

The technician placed a heavy metal mask over his face. The mask was cold and indifferent and crushing his ability to breathe. It felt like being suffocated by a machine.

He tried to convince himself that everything was fine, that he had to relax, that these people knew what they were doing, that he wouldn't asphyxiate inside the tight MRI tube, that he wouldn't die with this metal smothering his face. But there was some separate, autonomous entity inside him—his soul?—that had to get out and that overcame his brain's rationale for remaining. He made a frustrated sound and felt tears crawling out of his eyes and managed to say, "No, stop, please."

The technician removed the mask and said, "It's OK. It's OK."

He sat up, breathed, and apologized. "I'm sorry," he said. "I couldn't breathe. I couldn't—"

"It's OK," the technician told him. "You don't have to do anything you don't want to do."

"No," he said. "I know. It's just, I wasn't prepared for that. I didn't know. I think I maybe need some of the stronger... the stronger drugs."

"We can do that."

The technician smiled and Ed noticed that the technician had braces and he felt sorry for the balding, middle-aged man. The technician helped him up and led him out of the room, back to the kind nurse who smelled like Werther's Originals and who had already given him some Vicodin. They talked. She asked him if he was OK, what he was feeling. She was thin and had perfect skin and wore a gold necklace that glittered, and he wished she were his mother. She told him that neither she nor the technician knew anything about him or his condition; they only knew that the neurologist had ordered certain scans of his brain. She asked him what had happened, why he was there.

"Tell me," she said. "It's OK. There's no rush."

He tried to explain. He told her about the tumors and about his condition. His two potential conditions. And lately, he told the nurse, over the past six months or so, his hearing had started to deteriorate, and he felt like tumors were growing inside his head. He wondered if his failure was the fault of his ears or of his mind or of his brain, though he couldn't delineate the difference between these things. The only way to confirm the presence of tumors was to undergo an MRI scan of his brain.

"So that's why I'm here," he said. "I have to get this over with. I have to find out."

"I'm sorry," she said, then explained his options and put an IV in his arm. "This will help."

He felt lost and catatonic and as if he were being treated like a robot, but the reason he was here—his brain—was not a computer. He couldn't process everything. The nurse put her hand on his wrist to take his pulse. Her skin was as cold as metal.

As she led him back out to the MRI machine, his brain was far enough outside his body that he followed and obeyed and lay down where she indicated. This time, when the technician placed the metal mask on his face, his panic wore itself out and turned into a general, humiliated resignation that allowed him to sleep through the hammering, mechanical sounds that echoed inside the white tube as if a machine were trying to chisel into his skull, crack it open, see inside.

He awoke as the technician removed the mask from his face. The technician looked frightened.

"What?" Ed said. "You saw them? I have them, don't I?"

"I'm sorry." The technician mumbled, and Ed noticed that the technician no longer had braces. His teeth were perfectly aligned. It felt like maybe he'd been in the MRI for a year, long enough for the orthodontics to do their work. "I'm not allowed to say. I'm not a doctor."

"That means I do, doesn't it?"

"Here," the technician said, helping him up. "It's OK."

32

Whard they gave him the painkillers, he had to sign a
form vowing he wouldn't drive home. After he signed
it, he went to his car and started it and sat there, with his hands
gripping the steering wheel, lost in a hydrocodone haze. The
world seemed far away, too far away to manipulate, and he
couldn't fathom going home and dealing with Taylor, who
would want to know why he was acting so detached, like he
was high, like he was in one of her dreams. He couldn't see
her and love her and tell her what he now knew—or thought
he knew, what the technician hadn't quite told him. If he told
her, she would cry. She always cried, but even now he'd be
suspicious of her sadness, want it all for himself, and doubt
would distance them and distrust would seep in and something would keep growing inside his brain, something hard
and smooth and white and egg-shaped. A tumor. And inside
the tumor there was something black, as dark as heroin tar,
and it was going to hatch inside his brain, where it would
live, where it would overtake his brain and devastate it.

Ed sat in his car for a long time. It was almost winter again
and the days were mostly nights now and it was already getting dark. It frightened him and he had to escape. He headed
for the highway, for a road that led him away, elsewhere,
through a beautiful landscape that had been erased by night

and silence. Three hours later, he arrived on the other side of the Rockies, in a small city called Great Falls.

All he knew about Great Falls was what everyone knows about Great Falls: there's a bar with mermaids there. He stopped at a gas station to ask for directions. The bar, it turned out, was in a motel. He gave his ID to a steroid-swollen bouncer perched on a stool. Inside, the place felt as false and sinister as a plastic Halloween mask. It had a sort of twilight Polynesian theme. A roof of fake reeds extended over the bar and the booths in the back. There were no windows, and the carpet looked as black as a still lake at night.

In a booth with waist-high walls decorated with more imitation reeds, an old woman who reminded him of the skeleton from the opening credits of *Tales from the Crypt* played covers of classic country songs on an elaborate keyboard setup. Homemade backing tracks approximated the beats, and everything she played had a circus sound. Her voice wavered and cracked. She wore braces on both of her wrists. She played "Brown Eyed Girl" and a medley of Johnny Cash songs and "Fortunate Son" and she made every song sound the same, like they were all part of one endless, upbeat lament.

Behind the bar, girls swam behind glass, in a tank that looked like the deep end of a swimming pool. They wore goggles and orange earplugs and clips that pinched their noses and mermaid costumes that bound their legs. They waved to everyone and swam up for air and their hair spread out slow and followed them reluctantly. He had an impulse to go outside and call Taylor to tell her about it, but he knew he couldn't explain that this was real, that he was here, somewhere more exotic than her dreams.

Two men sat on stools and faced away from the mermaids so they could watch an Ultimate Fighting Championship match on a flat-screen that hung above the keyboard-playing lady. He sat down beside them and ordered a whiskey on the rocks and thought, *What sad weirdos come here on a Wednesday night,* before realizing that he was one of them—him and these UFC guys and a woman whose red hair was held back with a pink scrunchie and a man with a mayonnaise stain on the collar of his Air Force uniform and a party of eleven women, all drinking piña coladas with orange umbrellas, and a waitress carrying a tray of fishbowl-like glasses filled with an icy blue drink and a man who dropped his pants all the way to his ankles at a urinal in the men's room.

Then an Indian girl came in. She sat at the other end of the bar and started writing things on napkins, then pressing her messages against the tank glass for one of the mermaids to read. When she dropped one of her messages on the dark carpet, he surreptitiously picked it up on his way to the bathroom and read it in the safety of a stall. It said, *Everything will be fine.* It could be a clue. He put it in his pocket. *Plot,* he thought, *is just coincidence.*

When he returned, the girl was gone. A coaster covered the top of her full glass, and he felt like he'd allowed the world to get too far away from him, like he had to pull it back. He went outside and found her standing in the parking lot, surrounded by the motel, smoking a cigarette. He apologetically asked to bum one. She held her battered pack out to him and said, "Go for it."

She seemed younger than him, around twenty-four, around the age he thought of himself as still being. She wore an American Eagle hoodie and jeans and worn-down high-top basketball shoes and she was so thin that he already imagined that her hips were hard and skeletal and she had acne scars stitching her skin near her hairline but her hair was dark and full and cut into a neat bob and she had tight high cheeks and eyes that shied away from everything. She was still somehow compelling, and so her flaws were paradoxical and added to her attractiveness instead of diminishing it. A wisp of eyeliner extended the line of her eyelash.

"I feel like I've seen you before," Ed said. The cigarette quadrupled his drunkenness. "In Missoula." He felt like he was telling a fortune.

"Maybe," she said. "I've been there, but I live here." Like other Indians he'd met, her accent was defined by its absence. It made her sound unaffected and authoritative. She pointed behind him, toward the bar. "That's my cousin. The mermaid. But she gets bored in there so I write her notes. Talk to her."

He imagined being buried in liquid silence, communicating by napkin. He imagined the future. He looked at the girl and saw her eyes for the first time. He saw that there was a whole human inside her, dying to get out. There was one inside him too. They could help each other escape.

He wanted to say something but he didn't know what, so he said, "I was reading this thing online about how there's all these missile silos around here. Hundreds of them. For nukes, you know. For the Russians. In the Cold War. You could've ended the whole world from right here. If you just knew where the button was."

"It's true," she said. "They're all over, east of here." He thought of her cousin swimming in silence. "Do you want to leave here?"

Maybe if he went with her, desire could become some-thing. With Taylor, it had only consumed him. "Sure," he said. "Yeah."

Ed followed her to the street, around the corner and into a decommissioned police cruiser. Everything seemed arbitrarily sinister because it was inherently strange. He sat in the passenger side of the front bench seat. A white cat roamed around in the back, behind the Plexiglas. It was a big cage, but it was still a cage. Criminals had been in there. Along the dashboard there were empty spaces where equipment—a radio, a laptop, a radar gun—had once been. He complimented her car.

"It's nice, huh? It was my dad's. He was a cop here forever. But then, you know, he just had a heart attack and that was it. But the department gave me the car as a gift. Even though he didn't even die in the line of duty. Just to be nice, you know. To remember him by. It was nice."

He believed she was making it all up—the decommis-sioned car and the mermaid cousin and the cop dad and the trapped cat—but he couldn't find a way to dispute it, so he said nothing while she drove. The town was spread out and thin and it was hard to tell where it ended, but he knew they were outside it when she turned down a dirt road and onto another and then came to a stop. Her headlights lit up a small cabin that was spare and wooden and symmetrical.

"Here," she said.

She got out, slammed her door and let the cat out into the night, like she'd given it a ride out here to nowhere and was dropping it off. He got out, too, like she'd done the same for him. It snowed and the snow somehow impregnated the sky and the ground with dull light.

"What is this?" he asked, though he knew the answer.

"It's my grandparents'. They never come out here." She looked like she was dreaming. "No one does."

"Except us."

He felt her hand take his. It was cold like metal. She took a key from under a worn mat and opened the sliding-glass door. She led him in and flipped a switch. A bare bulb hanging on a chain from the ceiling lit up the space, which was, as he'd imagined, as spare as a Puritan chapel. The walls and floor and ceiling were all made of worn, hewn wood. A bed, just a mattress on a box spring, sat in a back corner. A black wood stove stood in the middle of the room, its chimney running straight through the ceiling. His breath made a brief ghost. He thought, *I could stay in here forever, away from everything.*

"Come on," she said. "It's freezing in here."

They went out back, and she led him to a stack of wood, where he found a hatchet resting on the snow like a murder weapon, like another clue. He watched her build a fire in the wood stove while he sat in a chair in his hat and jacket and gloves and waited for the room to warm up. The darkness made the windows mirrors, so he looked at the wood floor. A sluggish bug crawled across it. A fly. He didn't kill it. Then he saw another. Then another crawled by, slightly faster this time. He heard another one of them buzzing. She passed him a bottle of whiskey that he hadn't noticed. A new fly crawled across the sliding-glass door.

"There's flies in here," he said.

"It's warmer under the covers," she said and crawled in, fully clothed.

She looked like she needed him but he knew he didn't need her, so he took off his shoes and got in with her and lay on his back and looked at the ceiling. She cuddled close to him. She had removed her pants without him noticing, and he now felt the skin of her leg, which she'd laid over him. He felt the skin of her thigh and stomach press against his body. He'd been deceived into intimacy. She was warm, but he was warmer. He put his arm under her head and she put her head on his shoulder and she kissed his neck and he felt her ribs through her skin and she was a human who he could have without giving her anything. They had sex and he came on her stomach. It looked disgusting.

As they lay beside each other, the cabin grew warmer and she said, "We could live in here." Or maybe she said, "I could." He couldn't be sure. The static in his ears had swelled. "Away from everything," she said.

"Let's go to sleep," he said.

Sleep was the only way to escape. He was here with this girl who was looking for something she'd lost, and the elderly keyboard player from the mermaid bar was across town, asleep in her twin bed, in a nightgown as soft as snow, and the bartender was watching reruns of regular season football games on channel 430-something, and the bouncer was working his second job, unloading boxes at the airport, and the men who'd been watching UFC were alone in the motel now, and heroin addicts were passed out in parking garages, but his girlfriend lived outside his imagination, beyond his brain, inside her dreams. And here he was, burrowed away. *This*, he thought, *is what the inside of the Earth looks like: a hell you built for yourself. This*, he thought, *is a place to be dead.* "Goodnight," he said.

She whispered to him for a while, but he couldn't make it out. Then he felt her twitch and go slack, and he knew she was asleep. The cabin was silent except for a few flies flying around. He got up and sat in one of the chairs, with his back to the bed, and drank whiskey and fed the fire and went outside to get more wood. As the cabin warmed up, an entire civilization of flies awakened from their slumber. Spring had come for them within the hour. He had made it happen.

The glass of the cabin was lined thickly with their buzzing little bodies. It was like being inside a hive. As the buzzing accumulated, swelled, it only added to the static inside his head. It seemed cruel to kill them after they'd been resurrected, but the sound never reached a crescendo. It grew hungrily, unceasingly, like bacteria. He took some scrap newspaper that was meant for the fire and slapped at the windows. After the thud, bodies clattered to the floor, squirmed on their backs, kicked their broken legs. He felt guilty. It seemed like something that would happen in a quaint poem about New England. He slapped at them again. The same thing happened but to fewer flies. Then again—and again, to even fewer. And so on. As he killed them, they became harder to kill. They were ever more alert and elusive, but he was persistent and he killed hundreds of them.

Eventually he stopped and swept up their little carcasses and saw them in the metal dustpan and threw them out into the night. He thought of the Holocaust and knew it was the wrong thing to think. He tried to stop killing and to stop thinking, but it didn't work. The alcohol wasn't working either, so he sat down and did his best to ignore the flies. He failed. He killed more. There were maybe fifty left at this point. The fifty hardest to kill. It had something to do with evolution, maybe. He kept trying and trying, and he managed to kill a few more, before he gave up and stopped.

He lay on the floor, near the stove, and closed his eyes and urged himself to sleep, but the buzzing irritated him awake once again. He wanted to scream. The buzzing continued. His hearing came and went and seemed to return only when it was inconvenient or annoying. He laughed even though it wasn't funny. He sat up and swatted at the flies again and killed a few more, but the buzzing continued. He put his shoes on and went outside and stood in front of the cabin and turned on his phone. The screen said it was searching for service.

His pregnant girlfriend was asleep on the other side of the mountains and his phone couldn't find a signal, so he decided to sit there all night and wait for morning, until the girl he'd just slept with woke up and gave him a ride back to his car. He would drive back to his life and do better. Until then, he would sit there.

So he sat there, leaned against the sliding-glass door, in the middle of the enormous Montana night. His child was inside his girlfriend and his girlfriend was in bed, dreaming of him. Or so he dreamed, while flies buzzed against the other side of the glass, attempting an impossible escape.

33

He awoke in the night, from the cold and the need to pee. He peed a hole in the snow and went back inside, where it was bright and hot and flies flew around. He went to the bed where the girl slept curled up, with the covers tucked to her chin, and he saw that the girl was a girl. A child. Eighteen, at most. He'd been deceived. Everyone had: this girl, his girlfriend, and him. Shame surged through him and was converted into fear: he'd done wrong and, in so doing, he'd ceded his power to her, this girl whose name he didn't even know. He wondered how to wake her. How to be gentle and also to erase any trace of intimacy between them. He sat down on the bed, hoped his weight would wake her. It didn't. He matched his breaths to hers, which were slow and heavy. Would his child sleep like this child: smothered in unconsciousness? He thought of the MRI mask. He put his hand on her shoulder—on the covers that covered her shoulder—and shook her.

"Hey," he whispered. "Hey. It's time to wake up."

She opened her eyes and stared at something he couldn't see. "I dreamed I was a mermaid. A real one," she said. "Not in the bar." She closed her eyes, returned to her dream life, escaped the one where he lived.

He shook her again. "It's time to wake up. I have to go."

She opened her eyes again, looked at him. "Where? Where are you going?"

"To my car. You have to give me a ride."

"It's the middle of the night."

He looked out the sliding-glass doors. The sky was beginning to soften and gray. "It's almost morning." He couldn't look at her. "I'm sorry, but I need to go. I have to. Please."

"I'm sleeping. I will but I'm sleeping now. Come to sleep."

She lifted the covers, invited him in, and he saw her body. He saw the bones of it, she was so thin. He felt sick.

"I'm so sorry," he said.

He left. He walked through snow, to a plowed dirt road, and went the way he thought he should. It was as silent as sleep out there and he wondered if he were dreaming. He wasn't. He was going to walk the whole way, through the freezing hard night. He was going to perform an act of penance. To feel better, he would suffer. Ten minutes later, a sudden sunrise of headlights arrived behind him. The decommissioned police cruiser pulled beside him. The passenger side window rolled down.

"What are you doing?" the girl said. "Get in."

"It's OK. Thanks, but I'm fine."

"I got up. You woke me up. Now just get in."

He obeyed. The cat was curled up in the middle of the bench seat. He petted it while the girl drove. It purred.

"So what's the big rush?" the girl said.

"Work," he said. "I've got work." When he said it, he remembered it was true. According to the radio clock, it was 5:32. He was supposed to start baking at 7:00. He'd never make it. He'd have to call in sick. He'd have to lie his way back into his life. "I work early. I bake."

"What's your name?"

He made something up: "Jake. "

"Well I'm Kelly." She put her hand out while they drove and he shook it. "Nice to meet you."

"You too."

Then she laughed for an uncomfortably long time, like she was laughing at him.

"So when am I going to see you again?"

"Oh," he said. "I don't know. I mean, I live in Missoula."

"I know. Sometimes I'm down there. You should give me your number. Write it down."

"Sure," he said. "OK, yeah. That would be great."

He opened the glove box. There was a handgun inside. A handgun, several pens, and lots of paper. He thought briefly about gripping the gun—just for fun, just to show himself how reckless he was, but he didn't need to see that anymore, not now that he knew. He wrote down his number wrong, and tucked the paper into a cup holder. "There you go."

"Thanks. It was fun."

They were coming back into Great Falls. The streets were all empty and the buildings were all old. It felt like an abandoned movie set. When she pulled in front of the motel, he leaned over the cat and gave her a kiss on the cheek. He owed her something. Some solace or consolation. Some assurance. He'd taken from her and he had to give something back. "Talk soon," he said, then slammed the door and went to his car.

As he drove out of town and back over the mountains, the sun came up and revealed the world. The world here was sharp peaks, slow rivers, green pine trees, and blinding snow. It was all of this and it was him, in his dented sedan. He was the obvious flaw in the landscape. He passed through as fast as he could, stopping only for gas in the town where the Unabomber had lived and had been apprehended. While he filled his tank, he called his work and told them he was sick and couldn't come in.

"I'll spare you the details," he said.

He arrived back in Missoula around 8:00 and went directly to a jewelry store downtown. The ring his mother had given him no longer felt sufficient: he needed to pay to make his commitment become real. The store didn't open for two hours. He spent those hours in his car, with the seat reclined as far as it would go, not quite sleeping. When the store opened, he went in. A bell on a string *ding-dinged* behind him, to announce him. A thin woman appeared from behind a curtain, like a magician entering a stage, and offered to assist him.

"I'm looking for an engagement ring."

"How exciting."

He ended up spending eighteen hundred dollars on a thin gold band set with five small diamonds. He owed Taylor so much more than that but it would be a start. The rest, he resolved, he'd offer as the rest of his life. *Lucky her*, he thought.

When the saleswoman turned to run his credit card, he saw that her shoulder-length hair had been carefully hairsprayed to conceal a bald spot. It wasn't quite effective.

34

When he got home, the apartment was empty. He was alone and his phone was dead. He plugged it in. He had eighteen unheard voicemails. He didn't listen to them. He called Taylor and heard the panic in how she said hello. She said it like it was a question, like she doubted he was really there.

"Are you OK? Oh my God, I was so worried. I was sure something had happened. Something awful."

"I'm fine. I'm sorry. I just—"

He heard her begin to cry. He heard the release, the relief, felt her concern and felt awful. He apologized, assured her, consoled her, but none of it worked. He heard voices in the background. He asked where she was and she answered: "At the hospital." Her hurt, he heard, was turning to anger. "That's how worried I was. I was so scared. Where are you?"

"I'm home." Out the window, he watched someone try to negotiate a semi-truck into the Holiday Inn parking lot, in reverse. "I'm OK. I'll come get you and I'll explain."

Ed drove to the hospital where he'd had his MRI the day before. Taylor was waiting before the entrance, beside a bunch of people in wheelchairs. She looked so exhausted he barely recognized her. What he'd loved about her was her youth, her enthusiasm, and he saw that all that was lost, that he'd ruined her, and he thought that he'd have to repair her, since he would marry her, since she had his child inside her. But then she beamed when she saw him, and he recovered his feeling for her. The world can be so easy, if we'll let it be. Or so he thought then. She got in the car and they kissed. They hugged. They held each other. He idled illegally, in a handicapped spot.

"It's like you've been revived," she said.

She told him she'd been up all night, imagining the worst. She made him feel guilty. She told him that, in the morning, at dawn, she'd called the police and that the police asked how long he'd been gone and she told them all night and they said that wasn't long enough. Technically, the officer said, he wasn't missing. Just gone. It took seventy-two hours or something to make it official and initiate a search. But the police told her to try the hospital, to see if he'd been admitted. So she did and whoever she talked to—a receptionist or something—told her that, yes, actually, he had. He'd been admitted the day before. The receptionist would tell her this but no more. The receptionist said it was against the law. There were laws about privacy, said the receptionist.

"Isn't that stupid?" Taylor said. "So I went down there— here—to the hospital and tried to find you, to find out what happened, but no one knew anything or would tell me anything. And then," she said, "just before you called, I was on the elevator again and this woman was talking to this guy about a young guy who'd died. A young guy, they said, had been hit by a car over by Reserve, by the Wal-Mart, and he died. And so I asked them how old the guy was and they told me twenty-nine. So I started crying and they consoled me. The woman did. She said, 'It's OK, he's in a better place now.'"

Taylor said this and she laughed a little. "A better place? But you're fine, thank God. But where were you?"

"Nowhere. Great Falls."

He explained what he wanted her to understand. He wanted her to understand that he'd fled out of fear and that she should console him, forgive him, love him. That she should marry him, despite everything. It was difficult to explain, to make her understand. He told her about how he'd been having trouble hearing. He told her about the way sound was drowned out in static sometimes, about how it had been going on for a few months or more and that he'd wanted to tell her but didn't want her to worry. He told her that he feared the hearing loss might be caused by brain tumors, by the kind of benign tumors he had in his arm and his ankle. He explained that he thought it might mean he had the worse of the two conditions the specialist in Boston had told them about. He told her that the day before he'd gotten an MRI, to finally find out.

"I didn't want you to worry," he told her. "But I wanted to know. I had to, you know, because it's hereditary, the condition—my condition—and I was worried about, well—about, you know..."

"Our child?"

"Yeah. So I had the MRI and it was awful." He told her about the mask and the drugs and his suffering. "And when it was finally over—you should've seen the look on the technician's face. He looked so worried. Like he felt so bad for me. Like he'd seen something."

"Like what?"

"Like a tumor or something."

"But you don't know for sure, do you?"

"No, I mean you're right. Not for certain."

"But you don't really know?"

"You weren't there. You didn't see."

"I wish I had been. I wish you'd told me. I could've—"

"Could've what?"

"Could've helped you."

She looked away from him, out the window, at the world, at the crowd of people in wheelchairs, most of whom were now smoking cigarettes, strangely.

"But then, after the MRI, I felt awful. I didn't know what to think, you know, and I didn't know how to tell you."

"Tell me what?"

"You know. That our child, that he might have brain tumors, too. He or she."

"He won't. He won't or she won't—and neither will you."

"So I just went for a drive, to clear my head, and I kept driving. I drove all the way to Great Falls and my phone died and I just got a motel room, since it was so late by then, and that's all. I slept and came back this morning. I was just scared, I guess, but I'm sorry I scared you. I fucked up, and I'm sorry but what can I do? I love you."

She loved him too. He thought of proposing right then, in the front seat of his sedan, but it seemed wrong to do it there, in a hospital parking lot, so he suggested they go for a drive, for a hike. She agreed and they went.

The sky was solid blue, was as smooth as the inside of an eggshell, and he drove them through town and over the river, which had been frozen but was breaking up in the sunlight, and he drove them out of town, down a long road lined with strip malls and fast food restaurants and cheap hotels, the kind of road that's everywhere in America, except that here there were mountains in the background, which made the strip malls better and the mountains worse. As they drove, they talked about his hearing and his MRI and his condition and their child. They talked about how scared she'd been and about Great Falls. He told her about the mermaids and she told him about the people on the elevator, the people who'd consoled her so kindly. He apologized and she was forgiving. He explained his concern for his child and she assured him.

"No one's life can be perfect," she said. "And he'll be fine, just like you are. He or she. That's assuming you even have a brain tumor and that he inherits your condition. Which, who knows, you know? Just try not to worry. It'll be OK."

He felt better and so did she and he was taking her to a trail he'd been to once before. A beautiful place, the place where he would propose. They drove past suburban houses and kept going. They held hands. He turned left after a Wal-Mart. They passed ranch land. They passed goats and deer and they kept going when the road turned to dirt. He pulled off and parked at what he thought was the trailhead of a certain trail he'd been to before and together they started into the woods.

They walked over a creek and through a thicket of trees and came to a clearing that was littered with shards of glass and shot-up stumps and shattered neon-orange skeet, and he realized he'd never been here before, that he'd brought her to the wrong place, but it seemed too late already to turn back. There was a felled tree with bullet-riddled Mtn Dew bottles fitted upside-down over the ends of the branches. It was obviously an informal shooting range. They walked past it, back into pristine pine trees. They walked up a trail that climbed the side of a mountain. They walked up and up, went higher and higher. He looked at his girlfriend and thought, *You will be my wife*, and the thought startled him.

When they came to a scenic overlook, he did what he had to do: he looked at her and said, "I have to ask you something," then knelt down and took the ring box from his jacket pocket and proposed. You can do the right thing for the wrong reasons. "You've done so much for me," he said. Snow was soaking through the knee of his jeans. "Now it's my turn. I want to marry you and take care of you. You and our child."

Tears didn't well up in her eyes and spill down her cheeks. She didn't cry. She smiled, sheepishly. "Really?" is all she said. It wasn't at all like he expected. It was like all of life: a reminder of one's isolation inside one's own brain. "Are you sure? You don't have to."

"I want to. It's all I want."

She looked away from him for a long moment. "Then OK. OK, but not if you feel like you have to. Because you don't. You don't have to."

"I know. It's not like that. I want to, more than anything. Let's get married. Please: I love you."

She held her hand out and he put the ring on her finger and they kissed. They kissed, like they should. They told each other they'd love each other forever but she was cold and clouds were coming in and he said, "We should go."

They walked down the mountain, through the woods. They went back the way they came. They speculated about how surprised everyone would be, how happy they would be. As they neared the trailhead, they were interrupted by the sound of a gunshot ringing out in the canyon. Then another. Then another and another. It sounded like war but looked like the woods. It continued.

When the shots stopped, he called out "Hold fire" a few times but he thought it sounded like something someone who knew nothing about guns would call out, so he didn't yell as loudly as he could, out of embarrassment. When they hadn't heard a shot in thirty seconds or so, he assured Taylor it was safe to go, so they went. They walked up the trail and heard no more shots and came to the road, where two teenagers were leaned against a truck, pointing rifles at the ground, wearing hats.

"Hey," he said when they were close.

The teens looked at them like they were ghosts, like it made no sense for them to exist.

"You were up there?" one of them said. "Holy shit."

"We got engaged," Taylor said and showed him her hand, her ring.

This teenager who could've killed them was the first stranger to see it. This teenager congratulated them.

"Yeah," the other teenager said. He had dirty blond hair and a beard and wore sweatpants with holes in the knees. He had an unruly intensity. "You're lucky."

The way he said it, it sounded like a threat.

35

An Einstein Bagel had moved into the first floor of a newly built law office. A barbeque chain had moved in across the street. A Subway had moved into the bus depot, and a Jimmy Johns had gone in somewhere else downtown. A Cabela's was coming. The character of this place was being erased. The cause, of course, was a steady influx of outsiders, of people from the Midwest and the coasts, of people who wanted to leave Illinois but bring Cold Stone Creamery with them, of people like him. He loathed the change and he was the change, so he loathed himself.

He'd thought, idly, about moving to one of the many smaller Montana towns, such as Thompson Falls or Augusta, or declining cities, such as Great Falls or Butte. When he occasionally brought the idea up to Taylor, though, she wasn't interested. She'd grown up in a small, failing place and had escaped. Why would she return to one? "Besides," she'd say, "wouldn't going there just ruin wherever you went?" It was true. The only places he could go neutrally were Indianapolis and Houston, Charlotte and Sacramento. Cities like that, cities that were all suburbs already. Or seemed to be, from afar. So he stayed in Missoula. They stayed. They were going to make their lives there, have a family there.

They'd been engaged for a few days, and they went together
to see the neurologist about his brain. The neurologist placed
a black-and-white image on an illuminated wall light and
pointed with a pencil eraser to a tiny, ovular blur beside
his ear.

"There," the neurologist said. "That's what's causing you
problems. It's pretty small and I'm surprised it's had a notice-
able effect already, but there you go. There it is."

"Oh," Ed said. "Huh."

Taylor leaned in close. "It's barely anything."

Now they knew: he had a brain tumor and he had the
worse condition and he could pass it down to their kid.

"Now what?" Ed said.

"What about surgery?" his fiancée said.

"Whatever damage the tumor might do slowly, over time,"
said the neurologist, "surgery would do immediately and
definitely. It simply isn't worth it."

"So what do we do?" Ed said.

"You could see Dr. Kay again, in Boston. He might know
more, but I think he'll tell you the same thing: you'll just have
to wait and see what science comes up with. New advances
are happening every day."

Meanwhile, Ed thought, *I'm going deaf.* "OK" is all he said.

"For your other tumors, though, if they're causing you
pain, I can prescribe you something to reduce the discomfort."

Ed didn't want to leave completely defeated, so he left with
a prescription for hydrocodone. At least, he said to himself, it
was something. On their way home, they stopped at Safeway
and had it filled. When they get home, he took a pill, even
though none of his tumors were causing him any pain just
then. He took it to try it, to feel how it felt. He didn't tell her,

the woman he was going to marry, the mother of his future child. Warmth seeped through him, like dye dispersing in water. The warmth loosened his body, swaddled his brain. He lay on the couch, looking at the Internet and drinking coffee. On the Internet, he looked at the websites of young, contemporary photographers. Their subject was always *the mundane*. The style was always offhand. The websites were always spare. They made him feel calm, like the world was just something to look at.

His fiancée came and sat beside him and put her hand on his face and said, "Everything's going to be OK, you know." Then she signed *I love you* and gave him a kiss. She comforted him. She would make a good mother. "I gotta go," she said. She was meeting up with a friend for coffee.

When she was gone, Ed took another pill and then, later in the afternoon, he drank a beer. He had two. He thought it would all force him into a deep and nourishing sleep but when he lay down beside Taylor that night and she flipped her hair up so he could hold her closely and comfortably, his mind raced aimlessly and his heart beat hard and he finally got up and returned to the couch and the Internet and all night he skimmed through trivia. He discovered, for example, that there once was an expansion CFL team in Las Vegas called the Posse, which had accidentally drafted a defensive end who'd died in an off-season car crash.

Everything seemed irrelevant. It had something to do with the painkillers. The painkillers brought him deep inside himself and left him there, without a way out.

To facilitate his escape, he made a rule: in order to prevent himself from worrying and wondering about the abstract scope of his life, he was only allowed to think about the room he was in and about what that room contained. He went back to bed and tried to follow his rule.

It was night and he was in bed in the bedroom and he thought about how there was the mattress and the box spring and the sheets and the covers. There was the dresser and the clothes stuffed inside it. There was the carpet and the rubber tree they'd inherited from the previous tenants, who'd left blood and hair in the refrigerator and therefore may have been murderers but were probably just hunters. There was his fiancée, who was sleeping warmly beside him, against him. She didn't need him, he knew, but she would do anything for him. She was generous with her love and he was too consumed with himself to accept it. The thought kept him awake until dawn, unspooling its implications without ever unraveling them. His rule didn't work.

36

They went on a short vacation. They drove to the ocean. It was nine hours away. For the first time in his life, he saw the Pacific. For the first time in a long time, he saw an ocean. He thought about how he would die without accomplishing anything during his one time alive. It was all he ever thought about, when he wasn't thinking about sex. The ocean didn't have much to do with it. The ocean was maybe four-fifths of the world and it was all nothing. He stood on the edge of it.

"Let's go in," Taylor said.

They stood on the hard, dark, and damp sand that had been exposed when the tide went out before they got there. They took off their shoes and socks. She held on to him to keep her balance. It was cold, so they only went up to their ankles and quickly returned to the sand. Everything seemed vaguely symbolic. He felt nostalgic. What did it mean? That he was falling for something, for sentiment or something. He felt defensive. He'd be thirty in the fall. He'd spent his life so far, since high school, attempting to become ever more clever, and he'd succeeded and for what? He wasn't sure if the sound in his ears was the ocean or his encroaching deafness and he realized that his hearing loss sounded like an ocean, which didn't comfort him.

She said something that he couldn't hear and he said, "Sure."

They went for a walk and she talked and he nodded along without listening, much less hearing. It began to grow dark and he thought, *What a beautiful thing to watch grow.* She said something about going and they went. They walked over a dune and up a cracked walkway that ran between houses and brought them to a parking lot.

He started the car and said, "Now what?"

They pulled into the first motel they saw. It was vintage, kitschy, and Taylor ran in and discovered that a room would cost $128 a night, so they decided to leave the beach town and go to Astoria, the nearest city, where there would surely be more and therefore cheaper rooms, per the law of supply and demand. He drove. It was a dark, crowded two-lane road. All they could see were taillights and headlights and streetlights and stoplights and gas-station lights and other kinds of lights. He heard the ocean.

When a green sign welcomed them to Astoria, they began to look out for motels. They saw several and the No Vacancy neon of each of them was lit up.

"Well," he said, "I guess we can always sleep in the car."

"Shut up," she said. His brain returned to reception and he could hear again. "Relax. Look. There's a place."

It was called Hotel Seven and in cursive neon beneath the name, the sign commanded the reader to "Sleep in heaven," which sounded a lot like what the dead do. He pulled in and they went to the front desk together and were told that, yes, they had one room available. It had two queen-size beds and would be $132.

"Fine," he said, and when Taylor protested, he told her that it didn't matter. And it didn't: he had his secret savings. He said, "I'll pay," and acted like he was doing her a favor. She thanked him and he gave the receptionist his credit card.

The room was huge and depressing and they needed to eat, so he called the front desk and asked if there was a part of town where there were restaurants and bars and things like that. He meant a downtown but didn't say it. He meant that they wanted to find the nicer part of town—the part where cool young people like them hung out—but instead vaguely asked about food and drinks.

"Sure," the receptionist said. "There's the Pig and Pancake across the street." Ed looked out the window and saw it. It looked like a Denny's, except pink and brown. "It's a diner kinda thing. And then there's a Mexican place just a little past that."

They went to the Mexican place. It was expensive and mediocre. Families in which every member had blurry tattoos ate at the few other occupied tables. Now that he could barely hear, he barely talked. She looked like she might cry but she didn't. Instead, she ate her chicken enchiladas.

After they paid, they went back to their room and watched television, since she couldn't drink and therefore neither could he, not without her. They watched Animal Planet and a movie starring a girl from a CBS sitcom. In the morning, they had a disgusting and overpriced breakfast at the Pig and Pancake. While they ate, Taylor told him a story she'd told him before, a story about when a man tried to break into her house when she was eleven and she was at home alone for the first time and was dancing to some boy band song from early 2000s, was practicing the routine she and a Hispanic friend had choreographed to perform in the middle-school talent show. Sitting on her side of the booth, she sang a few of the lyrics, which had to do with the calculus of love.

"And I just looked up," she said, "and there was this guy with a cowboy hat and a handlebar mustache standing outside." She told him that she'd felt like she recognized the guy, like he'd driven slowly past her and her friends a few times while they were walking to school and had leered at them, and she was scared, so she ran to the doors and locked them—just before the guy could get to them. "I was scared," she said, "but it was weird: I just didn't really realize what was happening. What could happen. I didn't even call 911. I just called my friend Christine and she told me to get a butcher knife from the kitchen.

"So I was just standing there with the butcher knife and I looked at the guy and then he was gone. I thought I'd scared him off, I guess, and I just went right back to doing the dance to that song. But then," she said, gripping the imaginary knife and raising it up, "I saw that the guy was trying the windows and he got one of them open. Not totally open—just barely—but he was pulling up on it and I just screamed and then I called my other friend, my friend Monica, and she told her dad and they lived right around the corner and he was there in like five seconds, in his car, and as soon as he pulled into the driveway, the guy ran off into the desert. It was crazy. I just remember that handle-bar mustache, though, so well. He looked like a cartoon or something, to me."

Her life, he thought, was a story she made up for her own pleasure. He laughed but he didn't believe any of it. He believed she invented what she wanted. He said, "Why'd you tell me that story? What are you really trying to say?"

"Nothing," she said, defeated. "I mean, you haven't hardly said a word. I didn't just want to sit here in silence."

"Why not? What's so bad about silence?"

"Is this really how you want this to be? How you want your life to be?"

"Of course not."

"Then why are you making it like this? It could be different."

He looked at his plate and saw a breakfast sandwich smothered with the kind of cheese that comes with yellow nachos at baseball games and movie theaters. "I don't want this."

"You're such a child."

She ate her omelet and they left. He had a terrible head-ache. His brain pulsed inside his skull hard, like it wanted to hatch. He turned out of the parking lot and drove maybe five blocks and they came around a bend in the road and came upon a quaint downtown. They came upon bars and a boutique hotel and vegetarian restaurants and bookstores and people wearing fashionably distressed clothing and foreign cars parked at parking meters and flowers hang-ing from wrought-iron baskets and brick sidewalks. They'd driven nine hours and stopped five hundred feet before they'd arrived where they wanted to go. This was a critique of his impatience, he knew, but that didn't stop him from feeling angry rather than repentant.

"Are you kidding me?"

She began to laugh, like he was kidding her, and she continued to laugh. She laughed and laughed. "Oh my God," she said. "We came so far and never got here."

He drove through the town without stopping, despite her protestations. When they had escaped the town, he remembered that *Goonies* had been set there, in Astoria, and he thought that the whole world is a trap that lures you in with the idea that it will give you something. It's the way all traps work.

37

E d was engaged, was expecting a child, was nearly thirty, and he had a masters degree, if only in fiction writing, so he could've at least worked in a bookstore or tutored high school students for the SAT or that kind of thing but instead he mixed dough before dawn, baked bread in huge hot ovens until evening, and made nine dollars an hour. He baked, he'd told himself, in order to minimize his commitment to labor and protect his life from the world. He had to protect it to preserve it. According to this logic, he had to preserve it so that he could turn it into something else: fiction. So he'd preserved it but it had gone bad, as had his fiction.

He'd stopped writing fiction and he needed to make money. He needed a career. He had experience as a marketing assistant, from when he'd worked for the small press in Normal, Illinois, and as an assistant editor, from when he worked for a disreputable boating magazine in Chicago. He'd loathed both jobs but perhaps they qualified him for something sufferable. Maybe he could make something out of those five years spent sitting in Illinois offices. Maybe he could get a job in writing or in publishing or at least in an office. Maybe but how? There was a daily newspaper and a free weekly but he wasn't a journalist, so he Googled "missoula publisher."

The first result was for a company that printed Montana-themed postcards. The second was for something called Quote Unquote Publishing Consultants. He clicked. According to the About section, Quote Unquote Publishing Consultants was "a US developer of academic texts and reference materials." An address was listed. The office was right downtown, only a few blocks from his apartment, and he decided he'd print off a resume and walk over right then to see if they were hiring.

"What do I have to lose?" he asked Taylor.

"Yeah. Why not?"

So he went to the second floor of a historic building in the town's downtown and knocked on the frosted glass of an unmarked office door. It was like something done in a noir novel, except there was no intrigue. A harried-looking middle-aged man answered, invited him into a room that was more like a living room than an office. There was a white leather couch and a coffee table and a couple of modernist chairs. There was a table in the corner, cluttered with a computer, a printer, and all kinds of papers. There was seemingly only one employee.

"How can I help you?" the employee said without inviting him in.

"Is this Quote Unquote Publishing Services?"

"Consultants," said the employee.

"Oh." He tried to explain why he was here. "I worked in publishing," he said and named the press. "And I found you online and thought I'd stop by and see if you had any work."

"Good timing." The employee sat at the cluttered table. "Have a seat."

Ed sat in one of the modernist chairs. It was uncomfortable.

"I'm Sasha," said the employee. They shook hands. "Do you have a resume?"

Ed produced his from a backpack he'd had since high school, and Sasha looked it over, asked him general questions about his work history, his experience, and his education. Sasha had gone to the same Midwestern state university as Ed had, and Sasha asked him about various professors in the English department. Ed pretended to vaguely recognize some of their names, and Sasha reminisced about his senior thesis. "What was yours on?" Sasha asked.

"Flann O'Brien. The Irish writer."

"Oh, he's great. What's that one? *At Swim* Something Something?"

He thought, *Is Sasha the future of me?* It was a frightening thought: Sasha seemed so marginal, so mediocre, so alone in his office.

"So," Sasha said after their discussion of literature and college had petered out, "do you know much about what it is that we do?"

"Honestly, no. I just... I saw your website but that's all."

"The website?" Sasha laughed. "Well, basically, academic publishers hire us to make books for them. Reference books. Encyclopedias, mostly. Right now we're working on something called the *Encyclopedia of Terrorism*. The title's the best part of the book, unfortunately."

By the time Ed left the office, he'd been assigned to write a 2,000-word essay for a three-volume reference text on terrorism. The text would be published in the spring and sold to university libraries. He would be paid fifteen cents a word. The guidelines would be emailed to him.

When he arrived home that evening, the guidelines were waiting as an attachment in his inbox. They were exacting. The essay's contents were carefully prescribed. The subject was obscure: the Baader-Meinhof group. On his next day off from the bakery, he went to the university library and read.

According to his reading, the Baader-Meinhof group was named for a pair of revolutionary communists who lived in Germany after the Second World War. Baader, a man, set fires in Berlin department stores, in protest of the status quo. Meinhof, a woman, was a left-wing journalist who freed Baader from prison during a fake interview. They jumped out of a window. They escaped into East Germany and fled, using fake passports, to Palestine, where they trained with the PLO. Baader and Meinhof returned to Germany. Baader robbed a bank. Meinhof abducted her own children from her ex-husband and sent them to Palestine, to be raised in the training camp, but they were intercepted in Italy, en route.

Baader and Meinhof robbed a bank, bombed a train station, injured a police officer, and killed six more law-enforcement officials. They evaded capture and then were captured. Members of the revolutionary cell they'd started hijacked a plane and demanded that Baader and Meinhof be released. The hijackers were shot dead. Baader and Meinhof killed themselves, in despair. This was their despair: their suffering would be for nothing.

The essay Ed wrote told this story more slowly, with citations, and included a brief discussion of the group's historical context as well as a survey of contemporary scholarship that examined the Baader-Meinhof group in historical, political, and social terms. It was the first thing he'd written since abandoning his novel and it was so much better: it was about something real. Real suffering.

He emailed the essay to Sasha.

38

After the brain scan, Ed stopped thinking of his difficulty hearing as deafness and started thinking of it as hearing loss. He began to notice—or seemed to notice, at least, assuming there's a difference—that his hearing was worse in his right ear, near where the tumor was, than in his left. When he couldn't hear, he turned his head, in order to orient the right side of his head toward the source. Everything, it had turned out, was OK. It wasn't that bad. He could manage, at least until another tumor appeared inside his head.

He took two painkillers every eight hours and they killed the pain, deadened his brain. Thought was swaddled and slow. His hearing had continued to deteriorate and he was increasingly isolated within himself, which was an increasingly uninteresting place. His body was so slack with relaxation that he could rarely accumulate sufficient fatigue for sleep. He spent most of most nights on the couch, on his computer, and on one of these nights, he bought two tickets on a non-stop flight to Las Vegas with the money he'd made from the encyclopedia essay. The flight left in six days, on that Friday. After he bought it, he watched pornography on mute for a few hours but didn't jerk off because he didn't get an erection, which he blamed on the tumor in his sacral nerve. It was the same reason, he believed, he and Taylor hadn't had sex in five weeks.

At dawn, he went in the bedroom and lay down beside his fiancée. She flipped her hair up, so he could hold her. He held her.

"What do you think of Ken?" she said. "If it's a boy."

"I like it. I had an Uncle Ken." His Uncle Ken had died of cancer two years before. "He was the filmmaker. A really sweet guy."

"Come here, Ken," she said, practicing. "It's bedtime, Ken."

"Can we call him Kenny, while he's small?"

"Kenny? No. I don't like that," she said. "Just Ken. It sounds regular, classy, but it's not like Oliver or something. Sebastian. One of those trendy names."

"But maybe that's the next trend: regular names."

"Yeah. That's true. Everyone will be named Rick again."

"Hey, guess what I just did."

"Breathed," she said.

"Lucky guess—but no, seriously."

"Blinked."

"I just bought us tickets to Vegas. Plane tickets."

She turned and looked at him. Like everyone, she looked best in bed. "Why?"

"I've never been," he said. "I thought it would be fun. Get out of here, do something different. And I thought, maybe, if we want while we're there, we could just do it—just get married. Get it done."

"Get it done?"

"No. I mean, yeah. I thought that's what you wanted? To get married." He knew how it sounded. "I'm sorry," he said. "I just thought it would be good, before the child, to be married. And then later, we could still have a wedding. A big wedding with our family and everything. Like you want."

"You don't care what I want," she said, turning over and away from him. "It doesn't matter."

He protested.

"What do you think I want?" she said. She was sitting up in bed now. "Tell me."

"To be married," he said. "To have a child. I don't know." He went in to try to kiss her, to make things better, but she pushed him away. Pushed him hard. It was humiliating. "What's your problem?" he said. "You think I'm getting what I want? What do you think I want? A kid?"

"Fuck you. You're so fucking selfish." She was getting out of bed. She wore only underwear and a T-shirt. "I'm leaving. I don't know about this. I really don't know."

"I'm sorry, I'm sorry. Please." He reached for her hand, grabbed her wrist.

"Don't fucking touch me."

"I just meant I'm worried. I'm scared for the kid. That he'll have brain tumors, too. That he'll go deaf, too."

"You're not deaf." She looked at him like she hated him. "You're not. You hear everything I say. You just... I don't know. You want everything to be wrong, so you can suffer, so you can write some stupid short story or something."

"I stopped writing," he said. "I mean, I'm doing the essays now but not fiction, not like that."

She sat down on the bed and put her head in her hands, covered her eyes. He sat beside her. A child was inside her. The child had been in there for more than a month.

At this stage, according to a website he'd read one recent night, again unable to sleep, he or she looks like a tiny collection of tubes. But those tubes have important purposes! One tube is forming a brain and spinal cord. Another is developing into the baby's heart. Tiny buds on either side of the body will grow into arms and legs.

It was a process that couldn't be stopped. It was a frightening thought.

39

When Ed saw Kelly again, it was midway through the first period of a junior hockey game. When it happened, he had an animal response: his body stopped, for less than an instant. She was sitting in the front row, under a Pittsburgh Steelers blanket with a woman who could've been—and probably was—her grandmother. Ed sat with Taylor. They'd just taken their seats in the top row of the bleachers.

"Oh my God," Taylor said, "we're already losing."

Ed looked up at the rec-league scoreboard: Missoula Maulers: 0; Great Falls Americans: 2. Over eleven minutes had elapsed already. It was breast cancer awareness night, so the home team wore pink jerseys and laces. He looked at Kelly, who sat in the front row, ten rows away, and tried to convince himself that she was not her, the girl from the cabin.

This girl, she was too young, he said to himself. She was too ugly. She was too small. She had the wrong kind of hair.

But none of this mattered. Things do go wrong. He couldn't understand how he and Taylor had come in undetected, and he realized there was no way they could leave without being seen. There was only one un-alarmed entrance and exit, and it was on the far side of the 2,000-seat arena. The only way to get there, based on the current arrangement of spectators in the stands, was to clamber down to within two rows of

Kelly and her grandmother. Ed didn't know what to do, so he took a drink of the tall boy of craft beer he held in a souvenir koozie. Taylor drank from a can of sparkling water they'd snuck in, since she was pregnant.

"What the fuck?" Taylor said. "What the hell does that mean?"

Ed looked from Kelly to the ice and saw the referee blowing his whistle with one arm raised and bent in the air and his other arm pointing to it.

"Checking," Ed said. "Or high sticking, I think."

He took a long drink. He felt panicked. He stared at Kelly and prayed she wouldn't turn around. Meanwhile, kids ran beneath the bleachers and middle-aged couples yelled at the refs and the visiting team's coach paced along the bench and his players leaned forward against the boards, ready to leap into the game at any moment. As the seconds ticked down and Kelly didn't look back, Ed felt the dread and pressure accumulate inside him. It was like the opposite of an orgasm.

His plan was, when the period ended, he and Taylor would somehow escape, hidden among the many others who would also be getting up then. Once they were clear, he'd tell her they had to leave. He'd make up some lie about why. He'd say he was sick, he decided. That was his plan. It was the best he could come up with.

But the moment the period ended, Kelly stood, turned, looked around, and looked right at him. She looked thrilled. She looked like a teenager, he realized and remembered. She wore an Americans jersey but it was huge on her. Her fingers didn't even make it to the ends of the sleeves until she raised her arm, her hand appeared, and she waved.

He waved back.

"Who's that?"

"Her? She's a student. A former student."

"A student?"

"She was in my creative writing class."

"She was? Which one? What did she write?" Ed had told her all about the stories. The one about the "swamp people" of the Louisiana bayou. The one about a snowboarder. The rape fantasy. They'd laughed at the absurdity.

Kelly took long steps from bleacher to bleacher. She got bigger as she got closer. Ed's head began to throb with the increase of his heart rate.

"Oh my God," Kelly said when she arrived, standing above and before them. "I can't believe you're here." She acted as though Taylor weren't there. "I was going to call you. Promise. After the game." She laughed. "It's a sign."

"Hey." Ed felt Taylor looking at him, at Kelly. He said, "It's good to see you, but we have to go."

"Jake." Kelly put her little hands near her face, as if pained. "Why?"

"Who are you?" Taylor said.

Kelly looked at her, looked annoyed, and said, "Kelly."

"Who's Kelly?" Taylor asked Ed.

"A student," he said, looking at Kelly, trying to convince her. "A former student."

"Oh shit," Kelly said to Taylor, with genuine concern. "You're his girlfriend."

Taylor stood up, climbed down the bleachers, and pushed through people. As soon as she was gone, Ed went after her. He found her outside, alone in the snow-covered parking lot, just beyond a loose little crowd of smokers.

"Tell me," Taylor said, with genuine hate.

"What?"

"Right now. Tell me. That girl. Fucking tell me."

"Tell you what?"

Stalling only feels like an action. At that moment, it started to snow, very slowly.

"Just tell me that you slept with that girl. That teenage girl."

She looked like she might attack him and it seemed like that might be his only out, if she did and could then be made to feel like, *OK, now we are even.* So he told her, to provoke her. And also because what else could he do?

"I slept with her." He spoke softly, so the smokers wouldn't hear.

"With that *girl*. She's a girl."

"She's twenty."

"Are you fucking crazy? She's sixteen."

It was a point he couldn't argue.

"When? Just tell me when."

"In Great Falls."

"When I thought you were dead. When I was panicking because I didn't know where you were." In her expression, he glimpsed how he'd betrayed her, how he'd turned himself into a cruel stranger, insinuated his way into her life and deceived her. "We were in love," she said. "I have your child."

She turned and walked off, tearing at her hair, possessed. She left the arc of the arena entrance's light and disappeared into the parking lot's dark. He leaned forward, his hands on his knees, and he looked at the ground, the blank ground. He saw nothing. The snow had picked up, and he felt it melting through his T-shirt, cooling his back. He thought of all the warm mornings, of the white sheets, of the sunlight coming through windows, of walking together in winter, of car rides up bright and steep passes, of swimming at night. Everything, it was all gone. Where did it go? He began to walk home, but it was too slow. He ran home. He ran for miles.

He ran to their apartment's back door, but the back door was locked. It was locked, so he knocked. He knocked and knocked but she didn't answer, so he went around to the front door. On his way around, he saw a light on inside. When he arrived, he knocked again. Again, no answer. He knocked and knocked on the glass of the door. Behind the glass was a drawn shade. He knocked on the glass and called out her name.

"Taylor? Hey, I'm sorry." He knocked again. "Just fucking let me in."

He knocked harder and harder. He used the side of his fist and his wrist. He was furious with frustration, and his arm went through the glass. The glass shattered eagerly, like it had been straining to break, and the shards cut and bloodied him as his arm went through and again when he pulled his arm out and for a third time when he reached in to unlock the door and let himself in.

He let himself in and found her standing in the living room, holding a ceramic orange lamp in her hand. Holding it like a threat. "Get out," she said. "Go."

"I know you're mad—"

"Just get out. Leave."

He went to her. He walked slowly, with his hands out, apologizing as he went, as she backed away from him. She backed all the way through the apartment, to the tiny kitchen in the back. A kitchen the size of a closet. He trapped her there and said, "Please," and she swung the lamp at him. He grabbed it, grabbed her, and she slapped at him, hit him. She hit him and scratched him. She scratched him hard, like she was trying to rip him open, tear through him, like she was trying to get at what was inside, but he wouldn't allow her to have it. He fought back. He gripped her wrists and pulled her out of the kitchen, into the dining room, and pinned her to the dirty linoleum floor.

"Just stop," he said. "Stop."

He had her pinned to the ground and blood from his hands was smeared along the walls, was streaked along the linoleum, was splotched on her frustrated face, and he was telling her how much he loved her and how sorry he was and how crazy she was and this was when the cops arrived. They knocked solidly and announced themselves and then they just came in, with their guns drawn and aimed at him.

He put his hands up and tried to explain what had happened—that he'd cut his arm on the glass and that they'd gotten in a fight but that he hadn't hit her or hurt her and that this was all a misunderstanding—and Taylor told a female officer that she was pregnant, so they handcuffed him and put him in the back of a squad car, behind a plate of scratched Plexiglas, and one of the officers slid a little window open and said, "You're a piece of shit, you know that?"

"Yes, sir," Ed said. "I do now."

The officer shut the window, closed him in the cage of the backseat, and then his partner put the car in drive and drove him, locked like an animal, through the town's quaint downtown and beyond, past used car dealerships and grocery stores and casinos with liquor stores inside. As the world passed, it all looked so familiar and vague and gone, like a memory. He could never live there again, he knew, but he longed to. She lived there and their child would soon but he was here, with his hands cuffed behind his back, and he was going somewhere new. Somewhere unimaginably awful. When they arrived, though, the detention center, lit up by parking lot lights, looked like a suburban high school: low-slung, spread out, and built with those new grooved cinder blocks. The officer had to grip his upper arm hard when he led him inside. Otherwise, he might flee.

40

O ne guard took his clothes and assigned him beige scrubs and the same-colored slippers. Another guard explained the rules and the concept of *expectations*. Another classified him and assigned him a cell. Another told him that since Monday was Presidents' Day—a federal holiday—he couldn't be bailed out until Tuesday at 10 a.m.

"That's"—the guard looked at his wristwatch—"about eighty-some hours from now."

Ed said nothing during the entire procedure, just nodded along and resolved to endure his time in silence. In silence, he thought, it could just be time, instead of an experience.

The guard led him past cells containing humans who leered at him like they weren't even sure if he were worth their malice and who wore the same thing as him. His slippers slapped the concrete floor. The guard stopped him before the bars of a cell. An unseen observer—someone watching from a control tower or via a security camera—pressed a button that opened the door. The door's slow, mechanical slide reminded him of how a minivan's back doors move. Inside, it was as spare as the cabin where he'd been ruined. There were metal bunk beds and a stainless steel toilet, a bench, and a sink. Graffiti was carved into the walls, which were the color of curdled cream. A person sat up in the top bunk and said, "And who are you?"

The person was a thin old man with a mustache, a man who would've been an authority or an outlaw in earlier era but was just, say, an appliance salesman with a vodka problem in this one.

"What," the man said, "you too good to answer?"

He was.

The guard stepped out of the cell and watched the door slowly shut. Then Ed was alone with his cellmate, who lay back down, returned to his restless sleep, and Ed sat on the bottom bed, removed his slippers, and slept. He dreamed he was there, in jail, and when he awoke, he was. Nightmares are scariest while the threat is looming, lurking, while the threat is a still threat, before it arrives and you awake in a panic and realize it was all unreal. The threat there, in the jail, was violence—and Ed spent the next few days terrified.

He remained silent. He ate the food he was given. He stood against the fence and waited when he was allowed to recreate. He slept, and when he couldn't sleep, he lay in bed and considered the graffiti carved into the wall: a swastika, a crucifix, a crude drawing of a woman's ass, a good caricature of a cute poodle that was labeled *bitch*.

He wasn't allowed, legally, to contact Taylor, so he made one phone call to call his friend Dave. Dave had already heard what had happened from Taylor and Dave had enough to bail him out and Dave would be there Tuesday at 10:00 to get him.

"Good luck," Dave said. "I'll see you soon."

Dave hung up and Ed went back to his cell, and when a female guard came by with a little metal cart full of romance novels on Saturday afternoon, he took as many as he was allowed: five. He sat on his bed and he read all of them and then he started over. It was like being in a re-education camp for people who've forgotten how to love. He learned that all a woman wants is to be desired, that a woman can forgive any transgression, so long as it arises from passion. He felt hopeful. What had happened, though awful, was an outcome of his love. She would see that—or he would show her—and this would allow them to reconcile.

On Tuesday morning, a guard came and got him. When he returned the slippers he'd been issued, he was surprised by how unclean they'd become. The jail seemed so sterile but the slippers were dark with dirt. After he'd changed back into his bloody sweatshirt and jeans, another guard gave him his court date and explained that he wasn't allowed, legally, to contact Taylor for ten days.

"Violate that," the guard said, "and you'll end up right back here. OK?" The guard looked at him hard. "Answer me."

"Sorry," he said, speaking for the first time in days. "I understand."

"You might not belong here," the guard said, "but you're here and once you've been here, it gets harder and harder not to come back. Remember that."

His life had gotten away from him. He had to get it back. He went outside, where it was sunny and snowing. He looked up into the snow, saw it come down like scraps, scraps that would be assembled into a solid surface as soon as they touched down. He heard his name and saw Dave idling in the parking lot.

41

D ave took him home, to the house he shared with his sister and her boyfriend, a guy named Brad who grew weed in the basement and sold it from the living room. The sister and Brad were still asleep, and he and Dave sat in the kitchen, drinking coffee and talking.

"Look," Ed said, "I know how it looks. I'd think the same thing. I mean, you have to take her side. I understand. But just so you know, she was the one who hit me. She had a fucking lamp and was swinging it at me. I mean, I'm not saying I've been perfect or like I've done everything right but it's not like it looks. I didn't break down the door and beat her up. It was more complicated than that. I was the one bleeding, not her. I was trying to calm her down. That's all. I was trying to apologize. That's all I was trying to do."

"But she's pregnant."

"I fucking know she's pregnant." A bumper sticker that said "Cheney skis in jeans" was affixed to the refrigerator. A bunch of empty Kokanee cans were collected on top of the washer and dryer, which were in the corner. A bunch of dogs were barking outside, in the neighborhood. It was all so hard to talk about. "Look. I understand: you have to take her side. I don't blame you. I would, too. You should. You really should. That's what you're supposed to do in this kind

of situation: believe her. You have to. What else can you do?
You have to give her the benefit of the doubt. I mean, I took
women's studies or whatever." He laughed briefly, tried to
lighten the mood. "All I'm saying is, it's more complicated
than it looks. I mean, I obviously really fucked up. I panicked
and I wish I hadn't. I really fucking wish I hadn't. But that
doesn't mean I, like, beat her or I'm abusive or something.
I love her. I'd do anything for her to forgive me. Anything."

Dave had a beard and rectangular glasses and he looked
defeated.

"I just don't really know what to say," Dave said. "I mean,
I hear what you're saying—I do. But it's just, either way, don't
you think this just isn't a good sign? That whoever's fault
it is or whatever, it still happened and maybe it just means
it's not a good idea and, like, it might be best to just move
on." Dave got up and put out his cigarette in one of the cans
on top of the dryer. He hadn't even noticed Dave had been
smoking. "I know it's not that simple but maybe it should be."

"Is that what she said? She wants to move on?"

"More or less."

"Hang on."

Ed went to the bathroom, which was filthy, and looked
in the mirror for the first time since the incident. He saw
himself and saw a pink scratch mark on his left cheek and he
believed what he'd been saying: that they'd both done wrong,
that there was a way to reconcile. When he returned to the
kitchen, Dave was doing dishes.

"Hey man," Dave said, "I have to go to work but you should
feel free to hang out here. Take a shower, borrow some of my
clothes. Whatever you want. I told my sister and Brad you'd
be here. They're cool with it."

Dave went to work and Ed took a shower and Brad and Dave's sister were smoking a bowl when he got out and they asked him if he wanted to take a hit, so he sat down on the couch and he did. The weed was incredibly potent and he got incredibly high, too high to be around anyone, so he went for a walk. He walked over a pedestrian bridge that crossed over the railroad tracks that ran through town. He looked down. A train that was just two locomotives, each facing the opposite way, was below and wasn't moving. The train reminded him of his relationship with Taylor. He was extremely sad and extremely stoned. He knew then that they wouldn't get back together and he knew that he'd known but what did that matter? Knowing means nothing, not when you're in love, as everyone knows.

He walked to the Holiday Inn across the street from where she lived, from where he'd lived, and he got a room with a view of their apartment. He sat on the bed and looked out the window until, four hours later, he saw her walking down the front walk and he saw that she was showing. Her belly was round with their baby. He saw her go down the paved path that ran along the river. He watched until she was out of sight, then he waited for her to return. When, three hours later, she did, he waited for her to leave again. In this way, he spent his day: longing for her, just to see her. He wouldn't stop, he decided, until he had her back. Her and the child inside her.

42

E d walked along the river and through downtown. He walked under the train tracks, via a tunnel with sidewalks running along each side. On the sidewalk on his side was a man passed out, facedown, with a knife in a leather case affixed to his belt. He had to step over the man in order to pass him. He stepped over the man, emerged from the tunnel, went up some stairs, and entered a gentrifying neighborhood of bungalows and Subarus. He kept going past a memorial for a pedestrian killed by a drunk driver (*Jeannie Lee Kittredge: 1921–1997*), cut through a baseball field covered with crusty snow, passed some slummy apartment buildings and some pit bulls barking in a manicured yard, and arrived at Dave's house. Dave was sitting outside, at a picnic table, with his sister and Brad. They were drinking beer. It was 3:00 p.m. It was Tuesday.

"What's up?" they said when he showed up.

"You know, not much."

He joined them. They drank beer, they smoked a bowl with hash sprinkled on top.

"Yeah," Brad said. The whites of his eyes were pink. He wore a baseball cap advertising a local brewery. "My friend Ashley hooked me up. She's been out in Portland but then she just showed up with all this hash. I think she's gonna sell it and move to Austin."

"Cool."

"So, hey man," Dave said. "Have you heard from Taylor?"

"It's only been six days."

Everyone was silent and awkward. Everyone was too stoned to talk about something so complicated, so grave. They were all, except Ed, on their seventh or eighth beer. This was when Ashley arrived. She rode up on a bike. A cheap Murray mountain bike. She had blond hair and was pretty, so she reminded him of Taylor, even though she had a septum piercing and wore a black sweatshirt covered with patches from broken-up punk bands. She looked about nineteen. She was thin. She was eager with energy.

"What the fuck's up, motherfuckers?" she said with a smile.

"Nothing. You know, hanging out."

She sat beside Ed. It seemed too early for the sun to be going down already. It was getting cold and she was warm. She smelled like shampoo. Someone asked what she'd been doing and she said, "Sleeping. I just woke up a fucking half hour ago."

She laughed and so did he. It sounded like the life for him, avoiding the day. She drank a beer and told them about this girl Jessie who wanted to kill her.

"What did you do?" Ed said.

"Who're you?" Ashley said.

"I'm Dave's friend. Ed."

"Oh," she said, satisfied. "Anyway, Jessie's just this girl who's mad because she tried to fight me on Thanksgiving and I ended up busting her head open and she had to get like six stitches. Eight."

He felt like an idiot around her but he wasn't as fucked up as Dave or Dave's sister or Brad, all of whom had more or less stopped talking.

"Well this is fun." Ashley laughed, and so did everyone else. "But I'm gonna get going." She looked at Ed. "What are you doing?"

"Nothing. I don't know."

"You should come with me. My roommates are probably up to something."

They walked together. Dogs barked at them. The moon looked to him like an escape hatch but he wanted to be with her. Cars slowed as they passed, in order to see her. He felt how he'd felt before: he felt feeling swelling between them. He took her hand.

"What the fuck?" she said but she didn't let go.

Her house was hidden behind huge lilac bushes that lined the sidewalk. They pushed between the branches and arrived in a yard lit up by a streetlight. The yard was covered in the kind of ice you get on the walls of your freezer. They went inside. All sorts of stuff was all over the place. Bowls, cups, an overflowing ashtray, a box of cereal, a Razor scooter, an empty aquarium cloudy from the algae-thick water it formerly contained. All the lights were on but no one was around. A fat gray cat slunk down the stairs, then fled back the way it had come when Ashley started up. Ed followed after her, into her room. She closed the door and he stood there, unsure what was happening or how to respond.

"You can sit on the bed," she said.

"Really?"

"You act like you're fucking fourteen."

He sat on the bed and she sat beside him, lay back to look at the ceiling.

"So," she said, "what's your story?"

"My story? Oh, I don't know. It ends badly?"

"Aw." She sat up and pinched his cheek. "Don't say that. It's all gonna be amazing." Now she pecked his cheek. They sat there in silence for a second. Intimacy accumulated. She said, "So, do you want to get like really fucking high?"

"I do."

She went to her closet, got on her tippy-toes, and came back with a Tupperware container. From it, she removed a needle, a spoon, and a baggie twisted tight, holding a square of black heroin. It was just like how he'd seen it on YouTube. He knew what it was.

"Have you ever?"

"Never."

"But you want to?"

"I think so."

"It's good," she said. "You'll like it. It's not like on TV or whatever. You're not gonna fucking die."

"Well, that's a relief."

She laughed. She used a lighter to heat the heroin in the spoon. There was a violin on the dresser. In the videos he'd seen, the users had children they never saw or had never seen. Their children were stillborn, were in foster homes, were living with their grandparents in the suburbs, with their mothers in distant cities. Heroin was a drug for the lost, for those who'd lost. Heroin was for him.

She pulled the substance into a syringe and gave it to him. "Hang on." She found a single sock and tied it around his bicep. The sock did nothing. His veins were already obvious. Blood pumped through him. "Perfect."

He picked the vessel that would send the heroin to his heart. He pushed the needle against his skin and the needle burrowed into his vein, drew blood, reddened the dark drug. The metal fit his vessel exactly. The metal was cold inside him. It was the cold indifference of a machine but then he pressed the plunger and the drugs slowly entered his blood, his heart, and the drug warmed everything, overwhelmed his brain. He felt insane—it felt so exactly like love. Like love but not love.

43

E d woke up in Ashley's bed, in his clothes. It was a little after noon.

"I have to go," he said.

"Stay," she said.

They lay close. He looked into her eyes, which were the green of extremely clean and clear water. He kissed her forehead, put on his shoes, walked back to the Holiday Inn, got his car, and drove to a gun range, to attend a concealed weapons safety course. He was attending as a reporter, not as a student.

A few weeks before—before things went wrong—he'd pitched an article to the local free weekly about a local gun activist and enthusiast. He'd found out about the guy from a profile in the *Wall Street Journal* that his dad had forwarded him. He'd pitched the story to the weekly's news editor, despite having no journalistic experience, and hadn't heard anything and had forgotten about it until, on his second day at the Holiday Inn, his cell phone rang and he answered and the news editor asked him if he was still interested in writing the article.

"Something fell through," the editor said. The editor wanted eight hundred words by the end of the week. Ed would be paid a hundred bucks. "What do you say?" the editor said.

Ed agreed to do it. He didn't know anything about guns or journalism but he liked the idea of an assignment. An assignment is purposeful and he was at a loss about what to do. Now, he was going to meet the guy and to observe one of the many gun classes he taught. The class would provide a frame for the story. Or so he hoped.

He drove down a series of dirt roads and came to a gate and entered and drove further down the dirt road. He arrived at the classroom building a few minutes early. The building was from whatever school of architecture came up with the Missoula County Detention Center and the local hospital and many modern high schools.

Adults of all kinds sat at two-person tables that faced a laptop open on a podium and a PowerPoint presentation projected on the white wall. The laptop was being operated by a man who had slicked back hair and wore aviator glasses and had a cell phone and a knife but no gun holstered to his belt and who looked generally like an air traffic controller.

He took a seat in the back row, beside a guy about his age. They nodded at each other in acknowledgment. Ed noticed a teenage boy with Down's syndrome on the other side of the room, with a notebook open on his tabletop, and he worried about the teenager carrying a concealed weapon. Then he felt bad for worrying.

He took out a notebook and opened it and wrote down a brief description of what had so far happened: "Through a gate with multiple locks, down a dirt road, on the grounds of the Birch Creek Shooting Range, twenty-five or so people assembled in a windowless room. A golden retriever wanders through. A cute red-haired girl. Some middle-aged women. Men of all ages. Everyone has two books: *Armed Response* and

Gun Statutes of the State of Montana. A plaque on the wall assures that NO TAX DOLLARS were used in the building of the range."

Then the subject of his future article started the class by introducing himself and announcing that there were two reporters in the room and asking them to identify and introduce themselves. A thin woman with a big camera stood up and spoke eloquently about how she was in journalism school at the university and was working on a documentary project about the gun culture of western Montana. Then it was Ed's turn and he didn't even stand up and he said that he was writing an article about the instructor and his efforts to reform gun laws but he didn't really know what he was talking about and this came through. He ended by saying, "Or something."

The instructor, who Ed had been talking about, looked confused, even hurt, and then he moved on by asking everyone else to introduce themselves. Himself or herself.

A woman with feathery hair thought the Second Amendment needed defending. A guy's wife hadn't wanted guns in the house but she'd recently passed away, so now he'd bought one and wanted to know how to use it. A man owned a business that was between a strip club and two bars and there had been four attempted robberies in the past year, so he was here to learn more about his right to defend himself. The teenager with Down's syndrome said he was working toward a gun-safety merit badge. A woman with immaculate makeup had been assaulted outside of work and her husband had a bunch of guns, so she figured it was time she knew how to use them. The fresh-faced, red-haired girl he'd noticed in his notes just said, "I'm going to college next year, so my dad"—she looked at the man sitting beside her—"signed me up for this class."

The instructor began what would become a three-hour lecture by arguing for the necessity of an armed populace. He invoked a study conducted by a group called Jews for the Protection of Firearms Rights. They were based in Missouri and the instructor admired the work they were doing, especially their study of the causes of genocide. In every single nation in which genocide has been perpetrated, according to the instructor's summary of the group's study, the slaughter of innocents was preceded by two things: first, the government required that all citizens register their firearms, ostensibly to protect these same citizens from criminals; second, the government confiscated these firearms. The instructor was careful to say that this didn't mean, necessarily, that gun control causes genocide—but he did suggest that this was the only conclusion any sensible person could come to and he did imply that applying for a concealed weapons permit was a way of standing up to systematic, state-sanctioned murder.

Then the instructor lectured at length about gun laws, gun safety, and how to best use a firearm to deter *bad guys*. Then he opened two long black cases full of handguns. Everyone, the instructor announced, was now free to come up and handle the guns, so long as they abided by his four primary safety rules: assume the gun is loaded, check the chamber to ensure that the gun isn't loaded, never aim the gun at anything except an exterior wall, and keep your finger off the trigger until you're prepared to fire. Then everyone, including Ed, got up and went forward and formed a line and one by one made their way through the two dozen or so guns, picking them up, checking their chambers, pointing them at the wall, and pulling their triggers.

He'd only fired one gun in his life. It was a shotgun and he was in the backyard of a friend's lake house in Michigan and he'd shot aimlessly at a few clay pigeons, which didn't look anything like birds, and then he'd swung the barrel of the gun back and inadvertently aimed it at his friend, who yelled at him and darted away. Ed was embarrassed and scared and ever since he occasionally tried to imagine if he'd pulled the trigger and killed his friend, who worked in media relations for an art school in Chicago now.

Now he was holding a revolver in a shooting-range class-room in Montana and he unlocked the barrel and spun it and confirmed that it was empty of bullets and pointed it at the wall and aimed at white paint and the instructor's argument that the threat of violence enables an otherwise unattainable brand of radically active individualism—a defiant isolation-ism—made sense. A physical sense. He felt empowered, instead of just trapped inside himself. He pulled the trigger, fired at the wall, but the gun clicked as harmlessly as a pen and he put it down, disappointed.

Then he did the same with the next gun and the next one and a dozen more. Each time he pulled the trigger, he felt a thrill at the thin possibility that he was wrong, that the gun wasn't empty, that a bullet would explode from it, shatter into the wall, and that this would solve something, break open an escape. It hadn't happened but the next gun was a derringer and it was as small as a toy and it didn't have a barrel or a chamber and he couldn't figure out how to check if it was loaded and he was embarrassed to ask and so maybe it did have a bullet inside and he held it in one hand and angled it up at the ceiling and didn't pull the trigger and looked around and no one was looking, so he moved the gun back toward the heel of his palm and concealed it with his hand and put it in his pocket and walked out of that windowless room, into a day that had been smothered by clouds until it died and turned gray.

He looked back to see if he was being followed and just saw the red-haired girl, who was watching him and exhaling cigarette smoke that made a thick, round cloud in the mist. He wanted to invite her along but where was he going? He was going to embark on the kind of isolationist life a gun would engender. He didn't want to write the article anyway. He was going to go back up by Great Falls and find an abandoned missile silo and live in it, away from everything, along with the red-haired girl and their child, but the girl stamped out her cigarette and went back inside, so he left without her, alone.

He drove back down the dirt road, watching his rearview mirror for someone to stop him and have him arrested and sent back to jail. No one did. He drove back to the paved road but he didn't get on the highway that would take him back to Great Falls. It wasn't an escape he wanted anymore. He wanted to confront what he'd done.

He returned to his room in the Holiday Inn and sat on the end of the bed, considering the gun. It was a machine for making fear. He felt less like a victim already, even though it was empty. He put it to his temple. His brain, he thought, had done this to him, had brought him here, to this generic room, away from the woman who should've been his wife and the child who was due. His problem wasn't the tumors but the way his brain became their victim. Maybe he could change his brain with a real threat, rather than one it had elaborated. He put the gun to his head and pulled the trigger and death arrived, only to evaporate at the hollow click of an empty chamber, and now he was not a coward.

Now he left his room, went downstairs, and crossed the street, even though it had only been seven days since he'd been released from the detention center. New glass had already replaced the pane he'd broken. He knocked gently and waited patiently.

Taylor came to the door and his heart fell apart. Love razed whatever lies his brain had built. A plain fact asserted itself: he loved her and she hated him. She looked at him like a specimen through the glass. She looked appalled, aggrieved. She mouthed the word *Leave*, unless she said it and he was deaf to it. It didn't matter.

"Please," he said. "Please." He held up a finger to indicate that all he wanted was one moment.

She looked trapped. She turned the lock. She opened the door but didn't let him in. She wore a loose blue dress that showed her swollen stomach. He'd fucked her in that dress. When he'd fucked her, she'd given herself to him. She'd given herself to him and he'd taken advantage. He'd ruined the gift.

"You're not allowed to be here," she said.

"I need you." He'd rehearsed this, what he wanted to say, but now it sounded empty of all the meaning he'd imagined it would carry. "I know what I did. What I didn't do. And I can do better. You'll see. I'll stay away from you if you want, but you'll see. I'm different now. I was scared or something. I'm not now."

"I'm leaving." Behind her, inside, he noticed the liquor boxes duct-taped shut, the backpacks and suitcases stuffed with stuff. He noticed that the apartment looked ransacked, depleted. "So you can have the place back in a couple days, when you're legally allowed to be here."

"What? Don't. I understand you can't be with me right now but that doesn't mean you have to leave. I can still help you out. I want to."

"Look." She looked angry. "I'm having a baby—a fucking human—and I have no clue what I'm doing. I watch fucking YouTube videos about how to change a diaper. I'm going home. My parents will help me until I figure out what I'm doing. What to do."

"I'll come. I'll come and just be there and help, however I can." He saw her in a K-Mart parking lot, surrounded by the desert, hounded by the sun, pushing a cart full of Pampers. "I want to be there, for you."

The thought that crushed him was just this: that her life would be hard and that it would go on without him. He cried and she comforted him. She went to him and hugged him, held him tight while he wept. When he was done, he saw that she was OK and this hurt him worse, that she didn't need him. She pitied him. He was pitiful. He needed her. He covered his face with his T-shirt.

"I'll be in touch," she said. "This isn't goodbye. We'll talk."

"I know, I know. I'm sorry. I should go. You're right."

"OK." She put a hand on his shoulder. "It's going to be OK."

Then she was locking the door. He heard it click.

His car was parked around the corner. His checkbook was in the glove box. He went and got it. He hadn't looked at his account online in at least a week and wasn't sure how much, exactly, was in it but he wanted to get rid of all of his

money without writing a bad check, so he tried to be ambi-
tious but safe. He wrote a check for $81,000 and made it
out to her. He still had a key to their apartment mailbox. He
put the check in there. He locked it in there. Then he left,
the gun in his pocket.